Perfect Harmony

"California Dreams" titles include:

"California Dreams": Behind the Scenes

Hot new fiction titles:

Playing for Keeps

Perfect Harmony

Who Can You Trust?

Perfect Harmony

by Chelsea Brooks

COLLIER BOOKS
Macmillan Publishing Company
New York

Maxwell Macmillan Canada
Toronto

Maxwell Macmillan International
New York   Oxford   Singapore   Sydney

Collier Books   Maxwell Macmillan Canada, Inc.
Macmillan Publishing Company   1200 Eglinton Avenue East
866 Third Avenue   Suite 200
New York, NY 10022   Don Mills, Ontario M3C 3N1

Macmillan Publishing Company is part of the Maxwell
Communication Group of Companies.
First Collier Books edition 1993
Printed in the United States of America
10 9 8 7 6 5 4 3 2

Library of Congress Cataloging-in-Publication Data
Brooks, Chelsea.
Perfect harmony / by Chelsea Brooks.—1st Collier Books ed.
p.   cm.—(California Dreams)
Summary: Romantic entanglements and other disasters plague the
members of the rock band California Dreams as they pursue
success.
ISBN 0-02-041972-4
[1. Bands (Music)—Fiction.]   I. Title.   II. Series.
PZ7.B79149Pe   1993
[Fic]—dc20   93-12876

To Franco Bario

Perfect Harmony

Chapter 1

"**W**hat is the *matter* with everyone around here today?" Jenny Garrison asked, gazing around the cafeteria of Pacific Coast High. "Did the guys in the kitchen sprinkle love potion in the meat loaf or something?"

She set her lunch tray down on the table where her best friend, Tiffani Smith, was sitting. Tiffani's head was bent over a copy of the school paper, *The Clarion,* and her long, sun-bleached blond hair had fallen over her face. When Tiffani didn't respond, Jenny pulled back her friend's hair with one hand and bent down so that she was looking right into Tiffani's hazel eyes.

"Hello? Did you hear me?" Jenny asked.

"Oh—hi, Jenny." Tiffani blinked in surprise,

1

then smiled. "Sorry, I didn't see you standing there. What did you say?"

Sitting down next to Tiffani, Jenny began poking with her fork at the chef's salad on her tray. "I was just wondering why every person in this whole school seems to be talking about dating and meeting the perfect guy or the most fantastic girl."

She pointed a finger at Tiffani's paper. "Not only that," she added, "but practically everyone in here is reading this week's *Clarion* as if we were going to be tested on it. What's going on, anyway?"

"You mean, you don't know?" Tiffani asked, her eyes wide with disbelief.

"Obviously not," Jenny replied drily, brushing her chin-length reddish brown hair off her face. "Are you going to fill me in, or should I just give it up right now?"

"Here's the reason everyone is so hyped up," Tiffani said with a grin. "It's the new personals column *The Clarion* came out with this week."

Looking at the page Tiffani was pointing to, Jenny saw a series of boxed-in advertisements. "That's right. I remember seeing something about this in last week's paper, but I was working so hard on my history project that I totally forgot about it."

"Well, you definitely shouldn't miss out on it," Tiffani told her. "Some of the ads are a riot."

" 'Friendly alien seeks human female of the teenaged species to demonstrate earthling dating rituals . . .,' " Jenny read aloud from a box near the top of the column. She giggled, grinning over at Tiffani. "It's intriguing, anyway," she decided.

"Now do you understand why everyone is going nuts?" Tiffani asked. "Reading the column is like eating those candies you just can't have one of. I'm totally hooked! Look at this." She pointed to an ad farther down the page and started reading: " 'Surf's up! I'm ready to hit the waves with the girl of my dreams. . . .' "

"You're into surfing, too, Tiffani," Jenny put in. "Maybe he's the guy for you."

Tiffani gave a noncommittal shrug, crinkling up her nose. "I don't want guys to think of me as just another southern California surfing babe," she said. "I'm also into playing the bass guitar and lots of other things."

"I know what you mean," Jenny said, taking a bite of her salad. She and Tiffani both put a lot of time and effort into the band they were in, California Dreams. Jenny didn't think she could ever date a guy who wasn't interested in that part of her life. "I guess I'm lucky to have a boyfriend who likes rock and roll as much as I do."

Jenny smiled as an image of Sean Flynn's curly, golden brown hair and handsome green eyes popped into her head. They had been dating for over a month now, and Jenny felt closer to him every second. It was almost too good to be true.

Every once in a while, she still pinched herself to make sure that being with Sean wasn't just a dream.

"Hey, look at this!" Tiffani's excited voice broke into Jenny's thoughts. "I can't believe we didn't see it before!"

Jenny focused on the personal ad that Tiffani was pointing to, near the bottom of the page. " 'To my own special California Dream girl,' " Jenny read. " 'The sparkle in your brown eyes is all the Solar Energy I need. Your voice stays on my mind. Love, S.' "

"Wow," was all Jenny could say.

A warm tingle spread through her entire body as she took in the words, reading them over and over again. Jenny knew right away that the ad was meant for her. She was the only girl in California Dreams who had brown eyes, and Solar Energy was the name of Sean's band.

"That is *so* romantic!" Tiffani gushed, grabbing Jenny's arm. "It *has* to be from Sean."

"Wow," Jenny said again, her eyes still glued to the ad. A grin spread across her face—she didn't think she could erase it even if she tried. "A month ago, I never would have guessed that I'd be so happy now—especially after the way I joined Solar Energy and then changed my mind and came back to the Dreams."

Jenny had gone through a difficult time when she first began dating Sean. Her older brother,

Matt, who also happened to be California Dreams' lead guitarist, hadn't exactly been a big fan of Sean's. In fact, Matt had disliked Sean so strongly that Jenny and Matt had fought about it all the time, and the effect on their band had been awful. It had gotten so bad that Jenny had decided to leave California Dreams and join Sean's band, Solar Energy.

Now that she and Matt had worked things out, Jenny couldn't believe that she'd even considered singing and playing keyboards in any other band besides California Dreams. She and Matt were closer than ever, and when they played with Tiffani and Tony Wicks, the Dreams' drummer, it was amazing. Nothing made Jenny feel better than when the band got together to play.

Except, maybe, the way she felt whenever Sean kissed her.

"Well, obviously Sean is crazier about you than ever," Tiffani commented. As she plucked a lettuce leaf from Jenny's salad, her smile faded to a thoughtful look.

"What's the matter?" Jenny asked.

Tiffani hesitated before answering. "It's nothing really. I guess I'm just a little jealous that you *have* a boyfriend."

Tiffani's dejected expression made Jenny feel terrible. "I didn't mean to go on about Sean," she said. "But I'm sure you'll meet someone soon, Tiffani. I mean, you're gorgeous *and* you're nice. Half the guys at Pacific Coast High want to date you."

"Well, it must be the *wrong* half," Tiffani complained. "Lately I haven't met a single guy I have anything in common with."

Her gaze settled once again on *The Clarion*, and a glint of determination came into her eyes. "But I have a feeling all that's about to change. You're not going to believe what I did." She lowered her voice and leaned closer to Jenny. "I put a personal ad in *The Clarion*."

"You're kidding! I don't believe it!" Jenny grabbed the paper and began eagerly skimming the entries. "Which one is yours? Wait—no, don't tell me. I want to guess."

Jenny skipped over a few ads that had been written by guys. She ruled out one by a "ravishing redhead" and another by a girl who wanted to meet someone on the debating team.

"Ah-ha!" she said, pointing to an ad in the middle of the page. " 'I go for music, surfing, ice cream, sunsets on the beach, and guys who can make me laugh,' " she read. " 'If you think you're the guy for me, write back. Blondie.' " She looked expectantly at Tiffani. "That's yours, right?"

Tiffani nodded. "What do you think?" she asked, a slight flush coloring her cheeks.

"Straight and to the point. I like it," Jenny

said approvingly. "So when will you start to get answers . . . *Blondie*?"

"Shhh! Not so loud," Tiffani cautioned. She glanced around self-consciously. "Mr. Dempsey— he's *The Clarion*'s faculty adviser—said the replies could start arriving right away. He's going to set up anonymous boxes in his office for all the answers. That way no one but him will know the real identities of the people who wrote the ads."

"I can't wait to see what kinds of answers you get," Jenny said. "The guys are going to die when they hear—"

Tiffani grabbed Jenny's arm, a panicked look in her eyes. "You *can't* tell them! It's too . . . personal."

It hadn't occurred to Jenny that Tiffani would keep anything from the guys in the band. Matt, Tony, and Sly Winkle, the band's manager, were like brothers to her and Tiffani. But when Jenny thought about it, she realized that Tiffani had a point. "They probably *would* tease you a little about this," she agreed.

"A *little*?" Tiffani echoed, rolling her eyes. "That's the understatement of the year. You know how they are, especially Sly and Tony. They're already completely obsessed with girls and dating."

Jenny couldn't help laughing. Flirting *did* seem to be a top priority for both boys. Sly had even had a crush on Jenny, but she was pretty sure he was over it now that she was dating Sean. They were all just friends, but Jenny knew the guys wouldn't hesitate to tease her and Tiffani about their love lives.

"Don't worry—my lips are sealed," she assured Tiffani. She glanced toward the cafeteria entrance, then smiled as her gaze fell on two boys who were standing there. "Just in time," she added. "Don't look now, but here come Tony and Sly."

Both boys were cute—Tony with his chocolate-colored skin and muscular build, and Sly with his wavy, dark hair and impish grin—but at the moment, they seemed to be arguing about something. As they got closer to the table, Jenny saw that Sly was holding a copy of *The Clarion*, which he was trying to keep away from Tony.

"I saw the ads first, you bozo," Tony was saying. Balancing his tray of meat loaf in one hand, he grabbed the paper away from Sly with the other and rapped him lightly on the head with it. "Keep your hands off."

Sly shot Tony a look of mock insult as the two boys sat down across from Jenny and Tiffani. "Didn't your kindergarten teacher ever tell you about sharing?" Sly asked. "In case you hadn't noticed, *I* was reading that, too."

"*Was,* is right," Tony shot back. He took a

pen from his pocket and marked one of the ads, ignoring Sly, Jenny, and Tiffani.

"You two are hopeless," Jenny teased. "Don't Tiffani and I at least rate a hello?"

"Sure. Hi, you guys," Sly said.

"Yeah, hi," Tony echoed. The two boys shrugged at each other and then turned their attention back to *The Clarion.*

Jenny exchanged an amused look with Tiffani. "We're touched by your sincerity. I take it you've discovered the personals column?"

"You bet," Sly answered. "Since you refuse to see what a perfect match you and I are, I'm forced to take desperate measures." He grabbed his heart and gave the girls a melodramatic look. "You don't know how painful it is to make myself date other girls."

"Yeah, I can tell how much it hurts by the way you're drooling all over those personal ads," Tiffani teased, raising an eyebrow at him. "My heart bleeds for you, Sly."

"This is the dating opportunity of a lifetime!" Tony exclaimed. He let out a low whistle. "There must be over a dozen ads from girls who want to meet Mr. Right. Man, will they ever be relieved to find out that I'm their guy."

"Dream on." Sly glared at Tony. "Once these girls tune in to the irresistible Sly Winkle charm, *you* won't stand a chance."

Jenny shook her head as Tony and Sly both attacked the paper, circling ads that sounded interesting.

"Hey, check *this* one out," Tony said, jabbing his finger at one of the boxed-in entries. He cleared his throat and started reading: " 'I go for music, surfing, ice cream . . .' "

He didn't seem to notice Tiffani's gasp or the panicked look that came into her green eyes. "Oh, no! She doesn't sound like your type at all!" Tiffani squeaked out. "Right, Jenny?" Her eyes pleaded with Jenny to help her.

"Definitely not," Jenny agreed. She bent over the paper, trying to find another entry to distract Tony. "Here—this one sounds much better," she said enthusiastically. " 'I've lost my heart to a rock-and-roll renegade,' " she said, reading the beginning of the ad.

"Hey, that would be perfect for me," Tony said with a confident nod. He eagerly took the paper back from Jenny and skimmed the rest of the ad. "It gets better, too. 'Ever since your gig at Sharkey's, I've known that you're the perfect guy for me,' " he read. " 'Tell me you know it, too.' "

"The Dreams played at Sharkey's a few weeks ago," Tiffani said, naming the main teen hangout in Redondo Beach. "Do you think she means one of you guys?"

Sly and Tony looked at each other, then gave

each other a high five. "Yes!" they crowed at the same time.

Jenny held up a cautioning hand. "Other bands have played at Sharkey's, too," she reminded them. "She's not necessarily referring to any of the guys in *our* band."

"Are you kidding? It *has* to be one of us," Tony said. "I can feel it." He reached over for one of Jenny's notebooks and ripped out a piece of loose-leaf paper. "And I'm going to let her know right now exactly how perfect I am for her."

"That girl could just as easily be talking about the band's *manager* as about a drummer or guitar player," Sly pointed out. "And knowing the devastating effect I have on the opposite sex . . ."

"Naturally, you think *you're* her rock-and-roll renegade," Tiffani finished for him.

"Why not?" Sly ripped another sheet of paper from Jenny's notebook and started to write on it. "You might as well give up, Tony. We both know I can outclass you in a second when it comes to impressing girls."

"Yeah, right," Tony scoffed.

Jenny listened as the two boys continued to trade insults back and forth. Shaking her head in amusement, she whispered to Tiffani, "I don't know if these personal ads are going to work, but they sure are entertaining!"

Chapter 2

As Matt Garrison followed his girlfriend into the cafeteria, half of his attention was focused on Randi Jo's tall figure and the long blond braid that trailed down her back. The other half was still concentrating on the subject that had been preoccupying him all day.

"I still can't believe the Rockets are playing not one, not two, but *three* shows in this area," he said excitedly. "Three Saturday nights in a row at the Skydome. It's going to be great!"

Randi Jo shot him a look over her shoulder. "And guess who's going to be at all three. Actually, I don't have to guess," she amended. "You've only been talking nonstop about getting tickets to every show since you read about them in this morning's paper."

Matt came up next to his girlfriend and put an arm around her shoulder. "I can't help it if I'm a rabid Rockets fan," he told her. "I've been crazy about them since way before anyone else even knew they existed. It's great that they're finally starting to get the recognition they deserve."

Matt had been following the Rockets' career since he first saw them in a local club in northern California when he and Jenny were visiting relatives there. That was about five years ago, and Matt had made a point of seeing them play every time he visited his aunt and uncle since then. He had been psyched when the Rockets' first record came out, about six months ago, and one of their songs, "Mall Rats," became a big hit. It gave Matt hope that someday California Dreams would have the same kind of success.

"There's Jenny and everyone," Randi Jo commented, pointing to a table in the middle of the cafeteria.

As Matt followed Randi Jo over there, he noticed that Tony and Sly were both feverishly writing, while Jenny and Tiffani looked on. Matt had no idea what they were working on, but from the amused expression on Jenny's face, it was something funny. She smiled up at Matt and Randi Jo as they squeezed in at the end of the table.

"Don't tell me you two are as obsessed with the personals as everyone else around here," Jenny said, nodding toward the folded newspaper on Randi Jo's tray.

"Personals?" Matt echoed, staring blankly at the paper. "What are you talking about?"

"In *The Clarion*," Randi Jo explained with a resigned sigh. "We decided to start a personals column, and today's the first day it's out. I tried to tell you about it before, but you were so psyched about the Rockets that you didn't hear me."

She held out the paper to him, but Matt was still too distracted to look at it very carefully. "Uh-huh," he said. "Hey, did you guys hear that the Rockets are going to be playing?" he asked the others.

Tiffani nodded. "After listening to you rave about them for so long, I'm definitely going to go see them," she said. " 'Mall Rats' is a great song."

"*All* their songs are great," Matt said forcefully. "You're going to love seeing them live, Tif, I promise."

Randi Jo let out a sigh as she unwrapped her tuna sandwich and took a bite. "Why do I feel as if I've already had this conversation? Can we please talk about something else?"

Hearing the weary note in her voice made Matt realize that he *had* been going on about the Rockets for a long time. "Sure," he told her. "Sorry, Randi Jo."

"That's okay." Randi Jo looked eagerly

around the table. "Has anyone seen that new French movie that came out, *Deadly Relations*? It's about this professional singer—"

"Speaking of professionals," Matt cut in, snapping his fingers, "what's going on with the demo tape we sent out?" he asked Sly.

"Yeah, Sly," Jenny chimed in. "Did we hear from any record companies yet?" Even Tony stopped writing long enough to give Sly a questioning look.

About a month earlier, California Dreams had made a professionally recorded demo tape, which Sly had sent out to record agents, radio stations, and local clubs. Matt hoped that the tape would help California Dreams make a bigger name for themselves, but he knew that it took time to get results. After Sly sent out the demos, Matt had tried to put them out of his mind, but thinking about the Rockets' success made him want to get things moving for the Dreams.

"Nothing yet," Sly admitted. "But I'm sure we'll hear soon."

"I don't know. . . . Maybe something went wrong with the mail and no one got the tapes," Matt said, frowning thoughtfully. "It might be a good idea to start following up. This could be really important to our success, and I think . . ."

His voice trailed off as his gaze fell on his girlfriend. Randi Jo was sitting across the table, chewing on a bite of her sandwich. The way she was frowning at him, Matt had the feeling that he'd forgotten her birthday or something. "What's the matter? Did I say something wrong?" he asked her.

Randi Jo finished chewing and swallowed before answering. "Oh, no," she replied, staring moodily at him. "Not unless you consider it wrong to completely ignore everything I've said today. Didn't you even realize that you cut me off just now?"

Replaying the last few minutes in his mind, Matt remembered her saying something about a movie, but he'd been so caught up in his thoughts about the band that her words hadn't really sunk in.

"Sorry, Randi Jo. I guess I *have* been a little preoccupied with the Rockets and stuff."

Randi Jo gave him a look that seemed to say "Tell me about it." "Matt, I don't want to complain or anything, but"—she hesitated a moment— "does *everything* in your life have to revolve around music?" She brushed back her blond bangs. "I mean, I know how important rock and roll and California Dreams are to you, but *I* have interests, too, you know."

A wave of remorse came over Matt. "Sorry," he said again. "I *do* get carried away when it comes to music. Listen, we'll go see that movie you were talking about, okay?"

"It's not *just* that," Randi Jo said with a sigh.

"You weren't even listening when I tried to tell you about *The Clarion* before."

"You mean about the personals?" Matt asked, looking at her in confusion.

"That was only part of what I was saying," she said, frowning again. "I'm in charge of organizing a dance to raise money for the school paper—two weeks from Saturday."

"That sounds great! You're organizing the whole thing?" Jenny asked.

Randi Jo nodded yes. "It's going to be a lot of work, but it'll be worth it. The money will pay for *The Clarion*'s printing costs for the rest of the school year."

"I can help out," Matt volunteered. It seemed like the least he could do to make up for being such an insensitive boyfriend. "In fact, I'm going to make a promise right now, in front of all these witnesses."

He held up his hand in a Boy Scout salute and looked solemnly into Randi Jo's blue eyes. "I, Matthew Garrison, do hereby swear to show more of an interest in the things that are important to my girlfriend and to stop acting as if rock and roll is the only important thing in the world."

"But, Matt," Sly said, looking alarmed, "it *is* the only important thing—"

"*Sly,*" Tiffani cut him off, glaring at him. "Don't listen to him, Randi Jo. Count me in to help out, too," she offered. "Maybe the Dreams could play at the dance—free of charge, of course."

"That's a great idea!" Matt said. He was happy when the rest of the band agreed. For once, even Sly didn't seem to care about making a profit.

"Really?" Randi Jo said, smiling at everyone. "Great! Maybe I can set it up with Lowell right away—he's the paper's editor in chief."

She jumped up from the table and hurried across the cafeteria, returning a moment later with a thin, blond-haired guy who wore glasses. When he heard the Dreams' offer, Lowell didn't hesitate to agree.

"With California Dreams playing, we'll be sure to attract a big crowd," Lowell said. "Thanks a lot."

"This is the kind of solution I like," Matt said, grinning at Randi Jo. "We get to help you out *and* enjoy rock and roll at the same time!"

Randi Jo's blue eyes sparkled with pleasure. "Sometimes it's a challenge staying together when we're so different, but it's worth it. I guess we're living proof that opposites *do* attract."

Chapter 3

"**D**id Sly say what he wanted to talk to us about?" Jenny asked the following afternoon.

She leaned forward in the backseat of her brother's car to look at Matt, who was behind the wheel. California Dreams had just finished rehearsing at their house, and now she, Matt, Tiffani, and Tony were headed toward Sharkey's in Matt's car.

"All he said was to be at Sharkey's at four-thirty and that it was important," Matt said, glancing at Jenny in the rearview mirror.

"I wonder if he got us another gig," Tiffani spoke up from the front seat.

"Or maybe he heard from someone about the demo tapes we sent out. Wouldn't that be great?" Jenny added. She elbowed Tony in the side, then

19

realized that he wasn't listening. He was bent over a notebook on his lap, writing.

"Tony, wouldn't that be great?" she asked again.

He glanced up distractedly. "Huh? Yeah, sure . . . whatever," he said.

"You didn't even hear what she said," Tiffani accused.

"Who cares?" Tony retorted. "It can't be as important as solving the romantic problems of half the girls at Pacific Coast High."

Matt turned his head to grin briefly at Tony. "Still working on your answers to the personals?" he guessed.

"You said it," Tony answered, nodding. "I've already sent out most of my replies. This is the best one, and it will definitely knock the socks off the girl who wrote the ad." Bending over his notebook, he started to read what he'd written: " 'Rambo, Luke Perry, and Denzel Washington can eat their hearts out,' " he began. " 'If you're lookin' for a dude who's cookin', I'm your guy.' "

He flicked the notebook cover closed and grinned at his friends. "Pretty hot, right?"

Jenny wasn't sure what to say. To her, what Tony had written sounded . . . well, self-centered and stuck up. She didn't think she would want to go out with a guy who sent her that kind of response.

Still, she couldn't speak for all the girls at Pacific Coast High.

"That's very, um, interesting," she hedged. "What do you think, Tiffani?"

"Well . . . if you want to know the truth, Tony, it's a little . . . heavy-handed," Tiffani told him. "A little macho."

"Just a tad," Jenny agreed.

A defensive look came into Tony's brown eyes. "Well, I'm a macho guy," he said. "Besides, girls love that kind of stuff, right, Matt?"

"Matt's a *guy*, in case you hadn't noticed," Jenny cut in before her brother could answer. "That doesn't exactly make him an authority on the female psyche. Tony, take it from me: If you really want these girls to go out with you, you have to be more romantic, more . . . flowery."

"Definitely," Tiffani agreed with a nod. "You have to say the kinds of things girls like to hear."

"Such as?" Tony asked, raising an eyebrow dubiously.

Jenny thought for a moment. "Well, instead of just talking about yourself, show a little more interest in getting to know *her*."

"Yeah. Maybe tell her what it was about her ad that made you want to meet her. That will show her that you can tune in to what *she's* all about. Girls

21

want to know that a guy can be sensitive as well as macho," Tiffani added.

"They do?" Tony stared out the window, biting on the end of his pen. "Well, if you really think that's the way to go, I guess I could say something like—"

Suddenly, he broke off, and Jenny saw his eyes focus on something up ahead. "Oh, momma, talk about tuning in!" he exclaimed. "Check out that babe in the red Corvette. I wouldn't mind tuning in to *her* wavelength!"

"You're hopeless, Tony," Tiffani commented, following Tony's gaze. "Aren't you busy enough already, chasing every girl who put an ad in the school paper? You'll wear yourself out if you don't give it a rest."

"No way," Tony maintained, his dark eyes gleaming. "When the Tony Wicks babe radar starts bleeping, I can't ignore it. Can I help it if I'm the kind of guy girls go crazy over?"

Matt pulled to a stop at a red light and then turned around to grin at Tony. "You have to understand what a big responsibility Tony is taking on," he explained to Jenny and Tiffani. "Being a stud is a tough job, but *someone's* got to do it."

"Give me a break," Jenny muttered, staring out the window.

Up ahead, she spotted the red convertible Tony had noticed. It was two cars in front of them and in the next lane over. The driver looked a little older than they were, as if she might be in college. Sunglasses hid her eyes, but her long, wavy chestnut hair blew behind her in the breeze.

"Well, at least you have good taste," Jenny admitted. Just then, the car moved up a few inches, and she caught sight of a guy in the passenger seat. "Too bad it looks like she's already got a boyfriend—"

Jenny broke off as the guy turned in his seat. She immediately recognized the familiar, golden brown curls and handsome face. "Oh, my gosh, it's Sean!" she breathed, feeling her stomach twist into a tight knot. "What's he doing with that girl?"

She looked at her friends, as if they could tell her why her boyfriend was with another girl, but they seemed just as confused as she was.

Glancing toward the red convertible again, Jenny saw that the brunette and Sean were both laughing uproariously now. Jenny couldn't help feeling that somehow they were laughing at *her*. She was almost relieved when the light changed and the red Corvette sped off. She couldn't have taken watching them much longer.

Tiffani reached back to give Jenny's arm a gentle squeeze. "Are you okay?"

Jenny was in too much of a daze to even answer. "Did I see what I think I just saw?" she asked.

"You mean, was your one and only getting

cozy with another girl?" Tony asked. "I hate to say it, but it sure looked like it."

"You *could* try to show a little tact," Matt said, glaring at him.

Tony opened his mouth to apologize, but Jenny cut him off. "That's all right. You only said what I was already thinking," she said quietly.

"Hold it a second. Don't you think you're jumping to conclusions?" Matt asked. "There could be a million explanations for what Sean is doing with that girl."

"Right! Maybe he's working on a school project or doing something for Solar Energy," Tiffani added hopefully. "Besides, why would Sean write you that incredibly romantic ad in the personals if he's interested in someone else?"

Tony raised an eyebrow at Jenny. "I think I read that one. Something about how you're all the Solar Energy the guy needs, right?" He poked a teasing elbow in her side. "Tiffani's right. Any guy who would say that isn't thinking about chasing after another girl, Jenny."

"Maybe you guys are right," Jenny said, smiling at her friends. "Thanks for stopping me from becoming completely paranoid and unreasonable. I'm sure Sean will be able to explain everything the next time I talk to him."

She felt a little better as she settled back against the car seat again. Still, no matter how hard she tried, she couldn't completely erase from her mind the image of Sean's laughing face and the girl in the red Corvette.

"Are you sure you're okay, Jenny?" Matt asked as they walked into Sharkey's ten minutes later. "You've been pretty quiet since we saw you-know-who."

"I'm fine," she assured him with a weak smile. "Like you guys said, something totally innocent was probably going on. Thanks for asking, though."

Matt nodded and slipped an arm around her shoulder. Jenny was more like his best friend than his sister, but he couldn't help turning into an overprotective big brother when he saw her looking a little down.

He hadn't even liked Sean when Jenny had first started dating him. Now that he was getting to know Sean better, Matt had to admit that he was a nice guy—not to mention a talented musician. The fact that he seemed to be crazy about his sister had helped boost Matt's opinion of Sean, too. He just hoped he wasn't wrong in thinking that Sean was a decent guy.

"It's about time you guys got here," Sly called over from one of the booths. He waved them over impatiently and then slurped from the chocolate milk shake in front of him.

"What's going on, Sly?" Tiffani asked, as she, Tony, Matt, and Jenny all squeezed into the booth with him.

"This had better be good," Tony added. "I spend enough time *working* in this place. I don't always feel like coming here on my days off. Besides, you're cutting into my valuable time for answering personal ads. Now that I have the inside track from Tiffani and Jenny, I know exactly what to say."

Sly gave Tony a probing look. "Inside track? You're going to fill me in, right, buddy? I mean, it wouldn't be fair to—"

"Are you going to tell us what we're doing here?" Matt cut in. He really didn't feel like spending the whole afternoon listening to Sly and Tony talk about their dating crusade.

"Right. Okay, here's the story," Sly told him. "After you started talking about our demo the other day, Matt, I decided you were right about following up on the tapes we had sent out. So I made a few calls, and . . . guess what?" Sly turned a satisfied smile on the others, waiting.

"Someone liked the tape?" Matt guessed, leaning forward. "Who was it?"

"Chloe Krieger," Sly announced proudly. "Not only did she like our tape, but she's giving California Dreams a radio interview on KPCH."

"The school's radio station? That's great!"

Tiffani exclaimed, her beautiful eyes shining.

Sly nodded. "We're going to be on her weekly show, 'Rock Beat,'" he explained. "We'll play a song on the air, then do an interview and take calls . . . that kind of thing."

Matt felt a rush of adrenaline pump through him. "'Rock Beat' is a really popular show," he said. "And now, everyone who listens to it will know who California Dreams is."

"This will definitely make the Dreams sound more official when we talk to record agents," Jenny added.

"No kidding," Tony agreed. "Didn't 'Rock Beat' get written up in some magazine?"

Tiffani nodded. "*Teen Scene.* According to the reviewer, Chloe really knows a lot about music. Even though 'Rock Beat' is a school broadcast, I wouldn't be surprised if people in the industry have heard of it. You guys, I can't believe we're actually going to be on the radio!" she squealed, grabbing Tony's arm excitedly. "When's our interview, Sly?"

"Tomorrow after school."

"Fantastic! I don't know about you guys, but I want a milk shake to celebr—" Matt broke off suddenly and looked back at Sly. "Did you say *tomorrow* after school?" he asked. "As in, Thursday?"

"Yup," Sly replied with a nod. "Do you have a problem with that?"

A feeling of uneasiness settled in Matt's gut. "*I* don't have a problem with it, but Randi Jo might. Tomorrow's the day I promised I would help her shop for supplies and decorations for *The Clarion*'s dance."

"So? The dance isn't for another two weeks. You guys can go shopping anytime, right?" Sly said with a dismissive shrug.

"Just tell Randi Jo you have to reschedule," Tony added.

Somehow Matt didn't think it would be that easy. "I don't know. You saw how upset Randi Jo got yesterday. She's feeling really sensitive about the way I put my music ahead of the things she cares about. If I break our date, she might not understand."

"We can't rearrange the interview," Sly said firmly. "Chloe only does the show on Tuesday and Thursday afternoons, and she's totally booked for the rest of the month. She only managed to fit us in because someone else canceled on her."

"Besides, *you're* the one who was so impatient to get things moving for the band, Matt," Tony pointed out. "It's your own fault if the rest of us are all hyped up about it now, too. I really don't think we should wait."

Matt knew they were right. It didn't make sense to postpone their interview. Besides, he didn't *want* to put it off, even for a second. Being on

"Rock Beat" could be really important to California Dreams. He just wished he could be sure Randi Jo would understand that.

"Don't look now, Matt," Tony said, "but guess who just walked in?"

Matt shook himself from his thoughts and glanced over at the entrance. Randi Jo was standing just inside the double doors with three other people. Matt wasn't sure who the two girls were, but he recognized the thin, blond-haired guy. It was Lowell, *The Clarion*'s editor in chief.

When Randi Jo saw Matt, a smile lit up her face. She came over to his booth while Lowell and the two girls sat down at a table.

"Hi! I didn't know you guys were going to be here," Randi Jo greeted them. "We just finished a planning meeting for the dance. I can't believe how much there is to do! We have to make posters, decorate, get people to bring food and drinks, make sure there are enough faculty chaperons. . . ."

She broke off and looked at Matt. "You're still going to help out with the shopping and stuff tomorrow, right?"

"Actually, I need to talk to you about that," Matt began, taking a deep breath.

Randi Jo's smile faltered. "Are you saying that you *can't* help out?" she asked.

"Not at all! I still want to," he jumped in. "It's just that tomorrow's not going to be a good time.

Maybe we could do the shopping over the weekend or next week."

Randi Jo sighed, crossing her arms over her chest. "We just spent the last hour working out a schedule. If you can't go tomorrow, it really screws everything up," she said. "Besides, you *promised*, Matt. What are you doing that's so important, anyway?"

"Sly got the band an interview on KPCH, and the show airs tomorrow," he explained. "There's no other time to do it. Sorry."

"That figures," Randi Jo said, her expression darkening. "What you're really telling me is that, once again, precious California Dreams comes before I do."

"That's not fair," Matt said. He could feel himself getting defensive. "If we could change the interview, we would. This is a big step for the Dreams. The least you could do is try to be happy for us."

Sly leaned around Matt to add, "You can't expect us to give up—"

"To give up such a great opportunity for the band," Randi Jo finished. She shifted from one foot to the other, letting out a frustrated sigh. "How many times have I heard *that* before?"

Matt started to object, but Randi Jo just shook her head and said, "Never mind. Listen, don't worry about it, okay? I'll find someone else to go with me. See you later."

Turning on her heels, she walked to the table where Lowell and the two other girls from *The Clarion* were sitting. Her whole body radiated anger, but Matt was feeling pretty angry himself.

"It's not as if I deliberately planned to back out of helping her," he said, turning back to his friends.

"In a way, I don't blame her," Jenny said thoughtfully. "It must be frustrating to constantly feel as if the band is more important to you than she is."

"That's not true!" Matt objected. "But I'm not willing to jeopardize California Dreams' future just to prove that to Randi Jo."

"I don't get what she's so upset about." Sly shook his head in disbelief, stirring his straw in his milk shake. "Can't she see that this is the chance of a lifetime?"

Matt let out a sigh. "Obviously not," he said. "I mean, I understand that planning the dance for the school paper is as important to her as this interview is to us. I still want to help out with the dance, but I can't help it if 'Rock Beat' just happens to be on at the same time as when she needs to shop for supplies."

"She'll probably calm down once she has a

chance to think it over," Tiffani spoke up, giving him a sympathetic smile.

Matt raked a hand through his brown hair and slumped against the back of the booth. He hoped that Tiffani was right, but he had his doubts. Serious doubts.

Chapter 4

Jenny sat in the library, staring blankly at her open history book. It was Thursday morning, and she had a test that afternoon. The trouble was, whenever she tried to study, the image of Sean laughing with the girl in the red Corvette popped into her mind.

Ever since she'd seen her boyfriend with someone else, she had been completely distracted. The night before, she had jumped to answer the phone every time it rang, hoping it was Sean. But every time, she'd been disappointed. She'd even thought about calling *him*, but her pride had held her back. She didn't want to seem clingy and dependent—that was definitely *not* Jenny Garrison's style.

"I'm sure he has a logical explanation," she

murmured to herself for about the zillionth time. Then she let out a sigh. "At least, I *hope* so."

With a groan, Jenny turned back to her book. Obsessing about her boyfriend wasn't going to help her get a very good grade on the test. She tried to put all thoughts of Sean out of her mind and concentrate on the Civil War.

She was looking at a map of the Battle of Gettysburg when a soft voice spoke up in her ear. "Hi."

Jenny never would have thought that one, simple word could sound so romantic, but it sent a shiver up and down her spine. Turning her head, she found herself nose to nose with Sean. Each time she was this close to him, it was the same—everything in her mind went blank. She felt as if she could stare into his vivid green eyes forever.

"Hi, yourself," she said, tugging gently at one of the golden curls that had fallen over Sean's forehead.

"What's a beautiful rock and roller like you doing hiding your talents in the school library?" he asked. He sat down across from Jenny and let his books clatter on the tabletop. When he reached over to touch her arm, Jenny felt an electric current pass between them.

"Civil War," she said breathlessly. "I have a test."

He smiled at her, and Jenny blinked, suddenly

flashing back to the look she'd seen him give that other girl the day before. Now that he was here, she could finally stop worrying about that—as long as he explained everything.

"So, what have you been up to?" Jenny asked, trying to keep her voice light. "I haven't seen you in a while."

"We just saw each other yesterday morning," Sean said. He smiled at her, tapping his fingers on the inside of her palm. "Remember, you told me how I was the greatest boyfriend in the world because I put that message to you in *The Clarion*'s personals?"

Jenny laughed nervously. "Oh, right. I was so busy with the band yesterday afternoon, it feels as if a lot more time has gone by."

All of a sudden, she felt guilty for doubting Sean. He *was* the greatest boyfriend in the world. But somehow, she couldn't ignore the questions that lingered in her mind about what she'd seen the day before.

"How are things going with Solar Energy? Are you guys busy?" she asked. Maybe Tiffani was right, and Sean's band was the reason he'd been driving around with that girl.

"About the same as usual," he replied, shrugging. "We didn't get to practice yesterday, so I'm really ready to jam today."

Jenny waited for him to explain what he *had*

been doing, but instead he started telling her about a song Solar Energy was working on.

"I thought you guys were maniacs about practicing. How come you took yesterday off?" she persisted.

Sean blinked and looked down at the table. "I had, um, some errands to do and stuff."

Errands? Usually, Sean didn't let *anything* get in the way of the band, certainly not something that sounded as unimportant as *errands*. Was it her imagination, or did he seem a little nervous right now?

"Hey, I've got an idea," Sean continued. He took both of Jenny's hands and squeezed them, looking at her intently. "Have you ever thought about what your absolute dream date would be like?"

What was going on here? Jenny wondered. Why the sudden change in the conversation? "Is this some kind of trick question?" she asked, raising an eyebrow at him.

"No tricks, just treats," Sean said softly, his eyes brimming with emotion. "Whatever you want, we'll do it."

The look on his face was so sincere that Jenny could feel herself softening. "Did I do anything special to deserve this great treatment?" she asked.

"You don't have to *do* anything special, Jenny. You *are* special. Period."

Jenny melted under his gaze. "Okay, I'll think about my dream date," she said, grinning at him.

Her friends were right—anyone who acted so crazy about her *couldn't* be interested in another girl.

Could he?

"I can't believe I've been going to Pacific Coast High for three years, and this is the first time I've ever been inside KPCH," Matt said later that afternoon.

He, Jenny, Tony, Tiffani, and Sly had just finished carrying their instruments and amplifiers into the radio station. Now Matt set down his guitar case and looked around.

KPCH was located in a small suite of rooms at one end of the second-floor hallway. From the outer room where he and his friends were, Matt saw through a glass window to the brightly lit, soundproofed room where a guy with razor-cut hair was talking into a microphone. Records and tapes were piled around him on the counter near where he sat, and Matt could make out a series of controls built into the counter's surface. While he spoke, the DJ reached over with one hand to cue up a record on one of the two turntables, while the fingers of his other hand moved over the controls. A red ON THE AIR light was illuminated over the door leading to the studio.

"That guy must be C.J. the DJ," Jenny said, coming over to stand next to Matt. "He does a rap show before 'Rock Beat' every week."

Tony pointed to a second door, marked MUSIC LIBRARY, which led off the outer room. "I'd love to look around in there. I bet they have an awesome collection of tunes."

"You guys, I'm starting to get nervous," Tiffani said, biting her lip. "What happens if I say something dumb on the air? Everyone in Redondo Beach will hear me!"

The truth was, Matt felt a little nervous, too. He wanted to make sure California Dreams made a good impression. On the other hand, he didn't think that getting nervous would help their performance any.

"Don't worry about it," he told Tiffani, trying to convince himself as much as her. "We've played in public dozens of times. This won't be any different."

"Right!" Sly agreed, clapping his hands together. "Playing will be a breeze. And during the interview, try to pretend the microphone's not there. Just concentrate on talking to Chloe."

Matt checked his watch. "Speaking of Chloe, shouldn't she be here soon? It's already quarter past four. 'Rock Beat' goes on the air in fifteen minutes, and we still have to set up."

As if in answer to his question, the outside

door to the radio station flew open and a petite girl with short, spiky black hair flew in. Her black leather jacket was open, revealing a short-cropped red-and-black-striped shirt that she wore over black bicycle shorts.

"Hi, everyone. I'm Chloe," she said, dropping a pile of books on the chair just inside the door. "You don't have to tell me who you are. I saw California Dreams play at Sharkey's last week. You guys were awesome!"

In a flash, Chloe's jacket was on top of her books and she turned to greet everyone in the band. Her cheeks were ruddy, and her dark eyes sparkled with energy, giving Matt the impression that she never stopped moving. The smile she turned on him was so infectious that he couldn't help grinning back.

"Thanks. And, uh, thanks for having us on your show," he told her, holding out his hand. He felt oddly shy and self-conscious all of a sudden, though he wasn't sure why. "I'm Matt . . . uh, Garrison. I mean, Matt Garrison."

He groaned inwardly. *Brilliant, Garrison. Dazzle her with your amazing charm and wit. Now she's going to think the Dreams are a bunch of dweebs.*

But Chloe didn't seem put off at all. As the rest of the band introduced themselves, she was really friendly. Matt couldn't be positive, but it seemed to him that she kept glancing his way as he told them about her show.

"Before I transferred here, I did a rock show in my old school in L.A.," she explained. "There are tons of bands there, and I used to spend a lot of time in clubs, so I really got to know the music scene. . . ."

The rock-and-roll scene in L.A. sounded amazing. Hearing about it was so interesting that Matt completely forgot to feel nervous about playing live on the radio. Before he knew it, C.J.'s show had ended, and he and the rest of the band had set up their equipment in the DJ's booth.

"What's happening, Redondo Beach!" Chloe spoke into her microphone at exactly four-thirty. "This is Chloe Krieger, and you're listening to 'Rock Beat,' the rock-and-roll radio show that brings you all the scenes that make the scene. . . ."

The next half hour passed in a blur. Matt barely remembered playing "Kaleidoscope," California Dreams' newest song. All he knew was that one minute they were playing, and the next they were all sitting around Chloe's microphone for their interview.

He wasn't usually the most outspoken member of the band—Sly and Tony, and even Jenny, were usually much bigger hams than he was. But today, Matt found that he was a lot more talkative than usual. Chloe seemed to have a way of drawing him out—somehow she asked exactly the right questions to get him animated and involved. It was as if she knew instinctively which bands he liked and what his hopes for California Dreams were. Matt had never felt more exhilarated in his life.

"Has anyone ever told you that California Dreams sounds a little like the Rockets?" Chloe asked.

"That would be the ultimate compliment," he told her, brimming with pride. "The Rockets are my absolute favorite band. . . ."

Spurred on by Chloe's encouraging look, he launched into the story of how he'd been a Rockets fan since first seeing them in northern California years earlier.

He had known that being on "Rock Beat" would be good for the Dreams' career, but he never would have guessed that it would actually be fun, too.

No wonder Chloe's show has been written up in Teen Scene, he reflected. *She's a really good DJ.*

And pretty, he added to himself. *Definitely pretty.*

Sly's head swiveled back and forth as he watched Matt and Chloe volley comments and jokes across the DJ's booth to each other.

Talk about chemistry! Those two were so

wrapped up in each other that the rest of the band might just as well have skipped the interview part of the show altogether. "Rock Beat" was definitely turning into a two-person event today.

Glancing at Jenny, Tiffani, and Tony, Sly saw that they had picked up on it, too. Jenny was looking at her brother as if she had just discovered a side of him she hadn't known existed.

Who would have known that he could be such a flirt? Sly thought. Usually, Matt was a lot more shy than this. Then again, Chloe Krieger seemed to have what it took to bring out the hidden sides of a guy. Sly might have been interested himself if he wasn't already on the trail of a half-dozen girls who had sent in personals.

"How about taking some calls?" Chloe asked.

Sly could hardly believe it, but she actually tore her gaze away from Matt long enough to look at *all* of them for a brief second. For the first time, Sly noticed the phone resting on the DJ's desk. All five buttons were lit up and blinking.

"Sure," Jenny spoke up.

Chloe hit one of the buttons and spoke into the phone's speaker. "You're on KPCH, and this is 'Rock Beat,' with all the scenes that make the scene. What can I do you for?"

"I just want to say that I think California Dreams is the coolest!" a girl's voice exclaimed. She went on to ask Jenny and Tiffani whether they would ever consider playing in an all-girl band.

While the girls answered, Sly sat back in his chair, feeling pleased with himself. Getting this interview had been a great idea. It was obvious that people were impressed by California Dreams. If the electricity between Chloe and Matt made their interview even more interesting, so much the better. After today, everyone in Redondo Beach would be dying to see the band live!

After the first caller hung up, Chloe hit another button and said, "Hi. You're on the air."

"You guys were awesome!" This time it was a guy speaking.

"Thanks," Tony said, grinning around the D.J.'s booth at the others. "Did you want to ask us anything else?"

"Actually, I was wondering where my friends and I can go to see California Dreams play live?"

Perfect question, Sly thought. But then he saw Matt's hesitant expression, and he remembered. At the moment, the band didn't *have* any gigs scheduled.

"Well," Matt began, talking into the phone's speaker, "we don't have anything definite lined up. . . ."

Sly's arm reached out automatically to push Matt away from the speaker. He couldn't let Matt admit to the whole town that they didn't have any upcoming gigs—not on the air!

Leaning close to the speaker himself, Sly said, "Sure, we have a gig lined up, Matt, don't you remember?" He looked to Matt for support, but Matt was staring at him as if he'd lost his mind.

"For all of you fans who want to see California Dreams, their next gig is going to be a big one. . . ." Sly paused, frantically searching his mind for the right thing to say. "Two weeks from Saturday, they'll be the opening band for the Rockets at the Skydome."

He was surprised to hear himself make the announcement. He wasn't sure why he'd done it—it was just the first thing that had come into his mind. Shooting a quick look at his friends, he saw expressions of total shock on all of their faces.

"Great!" Chloe jumped in. "Once again, that's two weeks from Saturday at the Skydome. Show time's at eight, so if you want to catch California Dreams, don't be late!"

While Chloe went on to take the next call, the realization of what he'd just done hit Sly, and he sank his head into his hands.

He had just made a huge promise to every single person listening to KPCH, and he had no idea how California Dreams could ever pull it off!

Chapter 5

"**S**ly, have you totally gone over the edge?" Matt asked as soon as they got outside the school building after their interview with Chloe.

"You're not much to look at, but I used to think you at least had half a brain," Tony added. "Now I'm not so sure."

Jenny fixed him with a cutting stare. "You *know* we're not opening for the Rockets. Why did you have to open your big mouth and tell everyone in the whole town we're playing that gig?" she asked.

Sly's head was starting to pound from the onslaught of accusations. He held up a hand before Tiffani could pounce all over him, too.

"I had to say *something*," he said, leaning against the brick wall. "You know how music fans can be. One minute they love you, but if you don't give them a reason to remember you, *poof*—" he snapped his fingers to illustrate his point—"you're history. They forget all about you."

"You mean, it doesn't bother you that you made a promise there's no way we can deliver on?" Tiffani asked, staring at him in disbelief.

Sly had been trying not to think about that. But now that he was being forced to consider the consequences, the situation didn't seem as hopeless as everyone else was making it sound.

"You don't know for sure that we can't get that gig," he said. "It's not as if we've tried and been turned down or anything. And even though the Rockets are a lot bigger than we are, they're not superstars or anything yet. We could at least give it a shot."

Tiffani, Jenny, Matt, and Tony all looked at one another. "I don't know," Jenny said doubtfully. "The Rockets probably already have a band opening for them. . . ."

"Actually, they might not," Matt put in. "The ad I saw in the paper said that the opening band was still to be announced. But that doesn't mean we stand a chance with them," he added, turning to glower at Sly.

"You shouldn't have made something up like that, Sly," Tiffani added. "I say we go tell Chloe the truth and have her make an announcement over the air to correct the mistake."

"No way!" Sly objected. "If we do that, you guys might as well throw away your instruments right now. Your fans aren't exactly going to appreciate that they've been lied to."

Tony crossed his arms over his chest, glaring at Sly. "Well, whose fault is that . . . *chump?*"

"All right, so maybe I got carried away. Maybe I shouldn't have said anything about playing with the Rockets." Sly shrugged. "It seemed like the right thing to do at the time, and, anyway, what's done is done. What I'm trying to say is, maybe I *can* get us the gig. You have to at least give me a chance to find out."

He flashed his most winning smile, but his friends still didn't look convinced. "I *did* manage to get our demo tape made, even when all the odds seemed stacked against us," he added persuasively.

Sly watched closely as the Dreams all looked at one another again. When Matt gave a little smile, Sly knew he was off the hook.

"Well," Matt said slowly, "maybe we *could* give you a few days. . . ."

"*Very* few," Jenny added forcefully. "Today's Thursday. If you don't have the gig lined up by Monday, we're telling Chloe so she can make the announcement on Tuesday's show."

Sly was about to object, but one look at the others' faces told him that they weren't going to give him even a second more.

"Fine." Sly summoned the breeziest, most self-assured smile he could. "That will give me plenty of time."

Matt stepped out of his room and picked up the phone in the upstairs hallway. He started to dial Randi Jo's number, and then stopped and put the phone down on the hall table again.

Just call her, he told himself, letting out his breath in a rush. He wasn't sure why he was holding back. Ordinarily he would have called as soon as he'd gotten home to tell her about that afternoon's interview. But Randi Jo had been so sensitive about everything having to do with California Dreams, Matt wasn't sure she would even want to talk to him after the KPCH interview.

"That's the third time in ten minutes that you've picked up the phone and then not used it."

The sound of his sister's voice right behind him made Matt jump. He turned to see Jenny standing in the doorway of her room, an amused smile on her face. "Is this a new way of working out or something?" she asked. "Pumping telephones instead of pumping iron?"

"Yeah, I'm getting in shape for the wimpiest boyfriend pinup calendar," Matt joked. Then he let out a long sigh. "I can't believe I'm nervous about calling a girl I've been dating for over six months."

"I don't blame you," Jenny said with a knowing look. "After the way you and Chloe hit it off today, I'd be nervous about calling Randi Jo, too."

Matt blinked at her. "What do you mean?" he asked.

"Oh, come on, Matt. Don't tell me you're not attracted to Chloe. Everyone who heard the interview today could tell that there was something between you two. You were so busy going gaga over each other that the rest of us barely got a chance to introduce ourselves."

Suddenly Matt felt fidgety and uptight. "That's crazy!" he said. "So what if Chloe and I happened to get along? That was just a music thing."

"Um, sure. If you say so," Jenny said, backing off. She shot him a sideways glance, then scooted past him and down the stairs. "Well, see you later."

Why was she looking at him like that? Matt wondered. So what if Chloe *was* really cute? So what if she *did* know more about music than any other girl he had ever met? So what if talking with her *had* been exciting? That didn't mean he was interested in her as a *girlfriend*!

Matt shook his head. Usually Jenny showed amazing intuition where he was concerned, but this time, she was way off base. He wasn't about to start something with Chloe when he cared about Randi Jo as much as he did.

Breathing in a determined gulp of air, he picked up the telephone once again. This time, when he dialed Randi Jo's number, he stayed on the line until she answered.

"Hi, it's me," Matt said cheerfully into the receiver.

There was a short pause before Randi Jo said anything. "Hi, Matt."

The icy edge to her voice caught him by surprise. "What's the matter?" he asked. "Did you have a problem getting all the stuff for the dance? Listen, I'll be glad to go with you to pick up anything you still need if—"

"No, that's under control," she cut in. "Lowell went with me. We got streamers, balloons, poster board, markers. . . . The decorations are going to look fantastic."

"That's great," Matt said uncertainly. He frowned into the hallway. If everything had gone so well, why did Randi Jo sound so . . . angry? He had the distinct feeling that he'd done something wrong, but he wasn't sure what it was.

"Look, I'm sorry I couldn't go with you today, Randi Jo. It's just that—"

"Yup, the decorations are going to look *fantastic*," she cut in sharply. It was as if she hadn't even been listening to him. "In fact, everything's going swell—except for the fact that we don't have a band for the dance anymore."

Matt was totally confused. "What are you talking about? The Dreams are going to play. Remember, we worked it all out with Lowell on Tuesday?"

"Are you talking about *California* Dreams? That's who I *thought* was going to play, but I happened to hear on KPCH that the Dreams are opening for the Rockets at the Skydome that night. So I guess you guys decided that you were too cool to play for a dumb little school dance, huh?"

The hurt and resentment in her voice made Matt feel terrible. The dance! He had completely forgotten that it was planned for the same night as the Rockets' first show.

"Wait a minute. There isn't really a conflict," he realized. "It's all a big mistake, Randi Jo. Sly just made that up about us opening for the Rockets. We don't really have that gig."

"You don't?" Randi Jo said after another pause. "Are you sure?"

Matt was relieved to hear her voice soften a bit. "Positive," he reassured her. "At least, I'm *almost* positive. Sly's going to try to get us the gig, but we all know that his chances are zilch."

He waited for Randi Jo to lighten up, but she just sighed and said, "But what if Sly pulls a miracle and you *do* get to play with the Rockets? You can't just leave me hanging like this, Matt. I have to know for sure."

"Can't you wait a couple of days? By then we ought to know if—"

"That's not good enough," Randi Jo's voice cut him off. "If you can't make a definite decision right now, then I'll just find another band."

Matt tried once more to reason with her. "Just give us a few days," he pleaded. "You have to admit, if we *could* play with the Rockets, we'd be crazy not to. . . ."

"Is that what *Chloe* thinks?" Randi Jo snapped.

"What does *she* have to do with this?" Matt asked, staring blankly at the telephone receiver.

"Nothing. Absolutely nothing!" Randi Jo's voice shook with fury. "You obviously don't care about the dance, so I'll get somebody else. I wouldn't want you to play, anyway!"

Before Matt could get her to explain, she hung up on him. The loud buzz of the dial tone echoed in Matt's ear, but he was too confused to replace the receiver in its cradle.

"What is going on!" he muttered to himself. Why did his life suddenly seem so complicated?

Matt leaned back in the plush movie theater chair, trying to pay attention to what was happening up on the screen. He was having a hard time follow-ing the subtitles, but from what he could tell, some French guy named Philippe was trying to convince Celine, the movie's heroine, to divorce her husband and marry him. The movie had taken a lot of twists and turns—Matt had lost track of what was going on a while back. It was getting harder and harder to stay focused on the action.

Taking a handful of popcorn, he glanced next to him at Randi Jo's profile. Her face was il-luminated by the glow from the screen, and all her attention seemed riveted to the movie. At least she wasn't angry, Matt reflected. It had taken a lot of work, but she was finally treating him like a human being again.

He had had to call Randi Jo four times on Thursday night before he'd finally figured out that she was jealous of Chloe. And it had taken three more calls before he could convince Randi Jo that *she*, not Chloe, was the only girl he was inter-ested in.

That had been three days ago, and since then, Matt had helped plan what food would be served at *The Clarion*'s dance, shopped for more poster board and paints, and now gone to see *Deadly Re-lations*, the French movie Randi Jo had been dying to see.

"What's Celine crying about this time?" he whispered, bending close to Randi Jo.

Randi Jo wiped a tear from her cheek before looking at him. "Aren't you paying attention?" she whispered back. "Henri has threatened to take both of their children if she leaves him."

"Oh."

Matt turned back to the screen, but he still couldn't get very involved in Celine's dilemma. His mind kept wandering to the latest song California Dreams had been working on, "Over the Edge." Something about the guitar solo still bothered Matt, and he went over and over it in his mind, trying to pinpoint the problem.

"Matt, do you mind?"

Pulling his attention back to the darkened theater, Matt saw that Randi Jo was frowning at him. "What?" he whispered back.

"You keep tapping your foot on the floor. It's driving me crazy!"

With a sigh, Matt quieted his foot. He and Randi Jo had spent so much time together over the past few days that he hadn't had nearly as much time for his music as he would have liked. He frowned, trying to remember what it was that she had planned for tomorrow—something with Lowell, but he couldn't remember exactly what.

He tried to summon a little more enthusiasm for her plans. After all, he *had* promised to spend more time doing the things Randi Jo was interested

in—it was only fair. But somehow, he felt a little
. . . bored.

Concentrate, Garrison, he ordered himself.

Matt blinked, staring at the actors on the
screen. But instead of the red-haired French
woman, Celine, he found himself imagining a perky
California girl with spiky black hair, vibrant
dark eyes, and the most captivating smile he had
ever seen.

Chapter 6

Sly stood outside of Sharkey's, staring through the glass of the double doors. He saw that Matt, Jenny, Tony, and Tiffani were already inside, sitting at one of the booths.

It was Monday, D day. From the expectant expressions on his friends' faces as they talked to one another, he could tell that they were waiting for him to appear with news of whether he'd managed to secure California Dreams as the Rockets' opening band. He was late for the meeting, but Sly still hung back. After all, he wasn't the kind of guy who could admit defeat easily. How was he going to explain that he hadn't yet been able to get California Dreams the gig?

"Be optimistic," he murmured to himself. "It can't hurt to stretch the facts a little." If he could just act confident enough, maybe he could get the band to give him a little more time.

Taking a deep breath, he swung open the doors and breezed inside. "Hi!" he greeted everyone, plastering a big smile on his face. "How's it going?"

"That depends on you, Sly," Matt answered.

"Yeah," Tony said, nodding. "What's the news on getting us to be the opening band for the Rockets?"

Think positively, Sly reminded himself. "Everything's going great," he said, smiling around the booth. "I've made a lot of phone calls, gotten through to some people. . . ." He didn't think it was necessary to add that those people were mostly receptionists who wouldn't even put his call through to the people in charge of booking for the Skydome.

"Really?" Tiffani said. Sly was heartened by the impressed look on her face.

"Sure. Things are really falling into place," he told her with a knowing nod.

"What does *that* mean?" Jenny wanted to know. "How about giving us a few specifics, Sly? Did you get us the gig or not?"

"I've made a lot of progress," he hedged. "I think that with just a little more effort, I'll have it in the bag."

The dubious expression in Jenny's eyes told

Sly that she wasn't buying his story. "Give us a break," she said, rolling her eyes. "In case you forgot, our deal was that if you didn't get us booked as the Rockets' opening band by *today*, we'd tell Chloe and ask her to announce our mistake over the air. Admit it, you didn't get the gig."

Why was Jenny always the one to see through him first? He let out a sigh. "Okay, so I didn't get it—yet. But, you guys, we *can't* give up!" Sly begged. "If I have a few more days . . ."

"A deal's a deal," Tony cut in. "Besides, it was a long shot to begin with."

"We just don't have the right connections," Matt added. He looked around expectantly at the others. "So I guess we should get in touch with Chloe as soon as possible, so she can make an announcement on tomorrow's 'Rock Beat.'"

Tiffani nodded her agreement, and then turned to Sly and said, "Still, thanks for trying." She patted him on the back, as if he were some ten-year-old Boy Scout who hadn't gotten all of his knots right or something.

"I can't believe you're all willing to give up so easily," Sly muttered, shaking his head.

"Don't take it personally," Tony said. "You gave it your best shot, but . . ."

Sly stopped listening halfway through Tony's sentence. "Personally . . . personally," he repeated to himself, frowning. Why did that remind him of something?

"The personals!" Sly jumped to his feet as it came to him. "I was so busy trying to get this gig that I almost forgot—tonight's my first date from the personals!"

Jenny raised an eyebrow dubiously. "You mean, there's a girl out there who actually *wants* to date you?" she teased.

"Not every girl around here is as blind to my charms as you are," he shot back. "*Hasta luego,* everyone. I have to get moving!"

Jenny watched Sly take off. Then she turned to the others. "So it's decided, then? We talk to Chloe?"

"Definitely," Matt replied. "I'll track her down tomorrow before her show." With a laugh, he added, "It's a good thing Sly has a date. Otherwise, I doubt he would have given up so easily."

Turning to Tony, Jenny asked him, "What about you? Do you have any dates lined up?" She avoided looking at Tiffani, not wanting to bring up *her* personal ad in front of the guys. She'd have to find out about Tiffani's dating situation when they were in private.

"Do birds fly?" Tony countered. "As a matter of fact, my first date is tonight, too. Some lucky girl is in for the time of her life with the handsomest, smartest dude in southern California."

"Not to mention the most humble," Tiffani added, giggling. She turned to Matt. "Aren't you glad you already have a girlfriend, Matt? You don't have to worry about impressing anyone new."

Jenny looked to Matt for his reaction, but he was staring at something behind her. Swiveling her head, she saw Chloe Krieger come into Sharkey's with two other girls. Jenny didn't miss the way Matt's brown eyes lit up when Chloe waved to them. A few seconds later, the DJ appeared at their booth.

"Hi! It's good to see you guys," Chloe greeted them, smiling at Matt.

"Hi, Chloe," Matt said.

It was just a simple greeting, but Jenny knew her brother well enough to recognize the telltale signs—the flushed cheeks and the extra-attentive way he was looking at Chloe. Jenny didn't care how strenuously Matt denied it. He definitely liked Chloe more than just as a friend.

" . . . Wow. So you guys aren't really going to open for the Rockets?" Chloe was asking, with a surprised expression on her face.

"Not without a miracle," Tony answered.

Jenny had been so busy thinking about the attraction between Matt and Chloe that she'd barely heard her friends explain Sly's error to Chloe. Chloe kept nodding her head while she listened, her palms resting on the edge of the table. She seemed genuinely concerned about the band's problem, but Jenny found herself questioning whether it was the Dreams, or Matt, that the DJ was *really* interested in.

"We wanted to talk to you, so I'm glad you showed up . . . ," Matt told Chloe.

I'll bet you are, Jenny thought.

" . . . Since it doesn't look like there's any chance of us playing with the Rockets," Matt went on, "we were wondering if you could make an announcement on your show telling everyone about the mistake."

Chloe nodded slowly. "I *could* do that," she said. "But, you know, there might be another solution." She sat down next to Matt in the booth, her dark eyes sparkling.

"What's that?" Tiffani wanted to know.

"Well, I don't want to sound stuck up or anything, but *I* have a few connections in the music scene," Chloe began. "After the show got written up in *Teen Scene,* people started inviting me to private parties, and bands started sending me backstage passes and stuff."

"Cool," Tony said, looking impressed. "Let me know if you ever need a great-looking drummer to go with you."

"There are probably a lot of guys in line ahead of you, Tony," Jenny put in. "Like maybe a boyfriend or something?" She couldn't resist probing a little, but the embarrassed look on Matt's face told her that she'd gone too far.

"*Jenny,*" he said, shooting her a warning glance. "That's none of our busi—"

"It's okay," Chloe said. "Actually, it's a good thing I *don't* have a boyfriend right now. If I did, he'd probably get jealous about what I'm about to suggest."

She turned a bright smile on Matt. "I've got a couple of things to go to in the next week or so—a party at the Basement tomorrow night, a record opening for the Electric Swans. . . . Why don't you come with me?"

"Sounds great," Matt said, nodding with interest. "I mean, the Basement is supposed to be one of the coolest places in L.A." A look of uncertainty came over him as he asked, "But why do you want *me* to go with you?"

"I bet anything that some people connected with the Rockets will be at one party or the other," Chloe explained. "Considering all the people I've met in the industry, I'm sure we could find someone who could introduce us to the right people. I still haven't heard anything definite about the Rockets' opening band, and their first show isn't for over a week and a half. If we make the right connections, I really think California Dreams might have a chance."

"That would be great! I mean, think of getting to play with the Rockets *and* doing all that behind-the-scenes stuff with bigwigs in the music industry. I'm psyched!" Tiffani exclaimed, an excited look in her eyes.

An uncomfortable expression came over Chloe's face as she turned to look at Tiffani. "Um, I'm not sure it would be a good idea for a huge group to show up," Chloe began. "The kinds of people who can help us might feel put off or threatened if a huge group showed up. I think if Matt comes with me, that will be enough."

Matt grinned but then caught himself. He turned a questioning glance on Jenny, Tiffani, and Tony. "Is that okay with you guys?" he asked.

"I hate to be a total pessimist," Jenny put in, "but what if we *still* can't get the gig with the Rockets? Do you think it's a good idea to wait until the last second to tell people we're not going to be playing with them?"

"Have a little faith, you guys," Matt said. "If Chloe says she can probably get us the gig, I think it's worth a try. I mean, we'd be playing with the Rockets!" He held up his hands, as if that explained everything. "If you ask me, that's worth taking a chance for."

Seeing the exhilarated expression on her brother's face, Jenny knew she couldn't say no to him. Still, they weren't the only members of the band. "What do you think?" she asked Tony and Tiffani.

The two shrugged at each other. Jenny noticed the sideways glances they gave Matt and Chloe—obviously Tiffani and Tony had noticed the attraction between them, too.

"I guess it can't hurt to try," Tiffani told Matt, smiling.

"We're counting on you, man," Tony added. He gave Matt and Chloe the thumbs-up sign. "Let's go for it."

"Great," Matt said. "Maybe we can pull off this gig for the Dreams after all!"

Jenny met his smile with one of her own. If California Dreams could open for the Rockets, she'd be as happy as anyone. But something told her Chloe's plan was going to cause problems. Matt was still going out with Randi Jo, after all, and Jenny had a feeling that Randi Jo wasn't going to be thrilled when she found out that he was spending time with Chloe.

Taking another peek at Matt, Jenny sighed inwardly. *I hope my brother isn't getting in over his head.*

"Is Randi Jo around?" Matt asked Tuesday morning, sticking his head into the room where *The Clarion* had its office.

Mr. Dempsey looked up from the table where

he was going over a series of layouts with a student. With his full, dark beard and swarthy build, the teacher looked as if he would be more comfortable in hiking gear than in the button-down shirt and jacket he wore. Matt had never taken one of his English classes, but he knew that Dempsey's laid-back, informal approach made him a favorite at Pacific Coast High.

"Hi, Matt," Mr. Dempsey greeted him with a breezy wave. "I can guess who you're here to see." He flicked a finger toward a doorway to his right. *"The Clarion*'s ace features editor is in there, re-viewing copy for our lead story."

As Matt approached the other room, he felt his stomach tighten. He and Randi Jo had been getting along much better since he'd started spending more time doing the things she was interested in. She really seemed to appreciate that he was willing to let the Dreams take a backseat for a while. Matt just hoped she would understand that now the band had to be a priority again.

Stepping through the doorway, he caught sight of her immediately. Randi Jo was bent over some typeset papers on a desk, a series of lines creasing her forehead. Print from the papers had darkened the tips of her fingers and left a smudge on her nose. She was concentrating so intently that she didn't appear to notice him.

Walking as silently as he could, Matt angled

behind Randi Jo and covered her eyes with his hands. "Guess who?" he said softly.

"Matt!" Randi Jo pushed his hands away and flashed him a bright smile. "What are you doing here? I thought we weren't meeting until later on at Sharkey's."

"Yeah, well . . . that's what I wanted to talk to you about," he began, shifting from one foot to the other. "I'm not going to be able to make it."

Her smile faltered the slightest bit as she asked, "Why? Did something come up?"

Matt took a deep breath. He didn't know how to break the news to her gently, so he just spilled it out as quickly as he could. "You know I'd never do this if it weren't really important," he finished. "But once Chloe convinced us that we might actually have a chance to play with the Rockets, we knew we had to act fast. Sorry about the short notice, but we only just decided ourselves."

That wasn't the full truth. Matt could have called her the night before. But somehow he hadn't been able to get up the nerve to face her until today.

While Matt was speaking, Randi Jo's expression had become darker and darker. And as soon as he'd mentioned Chloe, her whole body had tensed up. Now she just stared down at the tabletop, with her jaw clenched and her lips pressed into a tight line.

"Say something, Randi Jo," Matt pleaded,

giving a gentle tug to a long strand of her blond hair. When she finally looked up at him, her blue eyes were cool and distant.

"What about helping me out with preparations for the dance?" she asked. "Are you going to have any time for that?"

Matt hesitated before answering. He hated letting Randi Jo down, but he didn't see any way around it. "I'll do whatever I can," he told her, "but for right now, trying to get this gig has to come first."

He waited for her to yell at him for making promises he couldn't keep, or for spending time with Chloe instead of her, or for *anything*. Instead, Randi Jo merely said, "Fine." Then she looked back down at the article she'd been working on.

Matt felt as if the temperature in the room had suddenly dropped to fifty degrees below zero. The two of them were standing in the same room, so close to each other that he could reach out and touch her. But at that moment, Matt felt as if they were light-years apart.

Chapter 7

Matt paused on the front steps of the high school and glanced around at the stream of students heading across the lawn to the parking lot. He didn't see Chloe in any of the knots of guys and girls, but she wasn't supposed to meet him here for another ten minutes, at quarter past three.

Tonight was definitely going to be a night to remember, he predicted. Later on, he and Chloe were going to a private party at the Basement, and before that, she was going to introduce him to some friends she was still in touch with from her old high school. Chloe thought that there was a good chance of running into someone who knew the Rockets. Even if they didn't, Matt was still psyched. They were bound to talk to a lot of people who were into L.A.'s rock scene.

Sitting down on the steps, Matt pulled the latest edition of *The Clarion* from his notebook and began flipping idly through it to pass the time. He'd been carrying the paper around all day but hadn't really had a chance to look at it until now.

Matt sighed when he came to a huge advertisement for the dance *The Clarion* was sponsoring. Perfect Wave was the band that would be playing. Seeing their name printed instead of California Dreams just reminded Matt of how he had let Randi Jo down.

I couldn't help it, he thought defensively, and stifled a bubble of frustration as he flipped ahead a few pages.

"Ah, the personals. Now *here's* something I can handle," he said, letting his eyes skim over the entries.

" 'Awesome football player still waiting for a certain cheerleader to notice him . . .' 'Looking for a guy who hates bean sprouts as much as I do . . .' "

He skipped over most of the ads, but one of them, about two-thirds of the way down the page, caught his attention and held it. "Wait a minute," he murmured. "This is for *me!*"

Zeroing in on the boxed-in square, he read it: *MG, you know who you are. You weren't there for me last week, but I know we can work it out. Be at the Redondo Beach Cineplex, Saturday night at*

8:00. Our happy ending will be better than anything in the movies.

Matt blinked. MG *had* to be Matt Garrison, and he was sure he knew who had written the ad: Randi Jo.

Could it be that she had forgiven him for not helping out with preparations for *The Clarion*'s dance last week? Sure, she *had* been pretty steamed with him today, but now Matt at least knew that she was willing to try to work things out.

Matt smiled as he read over the ad a second time. After all the problems they'd been having, it was nice to have something special to look forward to. In fact, he had a feeling that Saturday night was exactly what he and Randi Jo needed to get their relationship back on track.

"What's the story with Matt and Randi Jo?" Tiffani asked, Friday afternoon after school. "I saw them pass each other in the hall yesterday, and they barely said hello to each other."

Jenny finished shimmying into the velour minidress she was trying on at Peralta's, her favorite store at the Redondo Beach mall. "Randi Jo's mad at Matt and in a way I don't blame her. He *did* promise to help out with *The Clarion*'s dance, but now he doesn't have any time to."

"I guess it doesn't help that he happens to be spending every spare minute with Chloe Krieger,"

Tiffani said. "If I were Randi Jo, I'd be jealous, too."

"Matt swears there's nothing between him and Chloe, but if you ask me, he's kidding himself." Jenny shrugged and then turned to face her reflection in the dressing room mirror. "What do you think? Is it me?"

Tiffani nodded approvingly. "It's perfect! Sean is going to die when he sees you in that dress!"

"You think so?" Jenny asked. Tipping her head to one side, she gave herself a critical once-over.

The minidress she had on *did* emphasize her slender figure, and the rich, deep burgundy velour brought out the color of her cheeks and the red highlights in her hair. The dress was short, but not *too* short. It made the most of her long legs, and the scooped neckline really brought out the gentle curve of her neck.

"I like it," she decided. Then she bit her lip. "But is it the *perfect* dress for me? I mean, are you sure none of these other ones would be better?"

Jenny gestured to the discarded outfits that were strewn around the dressing room. She started to reach for a pair of blue silk shorts with suspenders, but Tiffani stopped her.

"Trust me. *Nothing* could look better on you than this dress," she assured Jenny.

"I guess you're right. I just want to make sure

everything is perfect for my date with Sean tomorrow night," Jenny admitted.

While she took off the dress and slipped back into her jeans and T-shirt, Tiffani began gathering up the other clothes and replacing them on their hangers.

"You are *so* lucky," Tiffani said, a dreamy look on her face. "I would totally die if some guy offered to make my dream date come true. What are you two going to do?"

Jenny herself could hardly believe that it was true. *"Everything,"* she said, zipping up her pants and reaching for her ankle boots. "We're going to ride those silly paddleboats they have on the pond at Rollins Park. Then we're having dinner at Chez Lefleur, and after that we're going to the beach to roast marshmallows. Sean's going to bring his guitar because he wrote a song for me that he wants to play."

Just talking about the date, Jenny could feel her cheeks flush with pleasure. "But before we do any of that, Sean says he has a special surprise for me." She smiled to herself as she reached down to tie her boots. "No one's ever done anything like this for me before," she admitted. "I can't wait!"

"Wow!" Tiffani hung the last blouse on its hanger and then said, "If this doesn't prove that he's not interested in that girl we saw him with, nothing does."

Jenny nodded. Sean still hadn't said anything to her about who the girl was, but Jenny wasn't upset about it anymore. It was obvious that the only girl he really cared about was *her*.

"Sean Flynn must be the most romantic guy on the planet," Tiffani said, breaking into Jenny's thoughts. "Do you think you could clone him for me?"

"What do you need with *another* guy?" Jenny asked, shooting Tiffani a teasing grin. "You already have *three* dream dates lined up."

Tiffani gave her a nervous smile. "I'll have to see about the dream part when I actually meet the guys. But I *am* pretty psyched," she admitted. "One of the guys loves music and dancing and just sounds . . . you know, nice. It's hard to explain."

"I know what you mean," Jenny said with a nod. "What about the other two?"

"Well . . ." Tiffani smiled, and her cheeks reddened slightly. "They both seemed amazing. I mean, the letters were all about how great they thought I sounded and about how they couldn't wait to get to know me better."

"That's great! So, in other words, they didn't use the whole letter to tell you that they're the new Rambo or anything," Jenny said.

Tiffani giggled. "No, thank goodness. But I did get a few letters like that."

"They were probably from Tony and Sly,"

Jenny said, rolling her eyes. "Those guys are hopeless."

"Nice, but not my type." Tiffani bit her lower lip and added, "I just hope one of my three dates *is* my type. I'm keeping everything anonymous until we actually meet. Date number one is tomorrow night, and the only way we have to recognize each other is that we'll both be wearing red carnations."

Jenny waggled an eyebrow at Tiffani. *"Oooh!* That sounds so mysterious and romantic. Red, huh?" She grabbed a pile of clothes and pulled back the dressing room curtain. "Come on. We'd better hurry up and find you the perfect outfit to go with it!"

Jenny could smell the salty sea air as she made her way down the path that led to the cove where she was supposed to meet Sean. She curved around a rock at the top of a bluff and then paused as the Pacific Ocean came into view. The sun, sinking toward the horizon, was a deep red globe that sent ribbons of orange, purple, and yellow across the sky and sparkling highlights over the waves below.

"Wow. Talk about the perfect way to start the perfect date," Jenny murmured aloud.

She stared at the view and then closed her eyes in order to commit the image to memory. Tonight was going to be really special—she could feel it—

and she wanted to remember every detail.

Her whole body tingled with anticipation as she went down the rocky slope to the beach below. When she reached the cove, she didn't see Sean's familiar silhouette. She *was* a few minutes early, though. He was probably somewhere nearby, waiting for just the right moment to spring his surprise.

Tiffani was right, Jenny thought. Sean *was* the most romantic guy on the planet. She looked down at her velour dress. In the rich light from the setting sun, the color looked more vibrant and alive than ever. But it couldn't begin to match how alive she felt inside.

She tried to imagine what Sean would look like when he appeared, what he'd be wearing, what his surprise would be. But she simply couldn't.

"Don't even try," she told herself. "Whatever you think up can't possibly be as special as what he has planned."

Jenny was so excited that she practically bounced across the sand to a rock that she could sit on. Settling against the smooth stone, she closed her eyes and waited for the magic to begin.

"May I help you, miss?" The maître d' at Emilio's met Tiffani at the restaurant door, an inquisitive smile on his round, jovial face.

"I'm meeting someone for dinner," Tiffani told him. She swallowed a bubble of nervousness and gazed around the restaurant's interior.

Emilio's was a family-style Italian restaurant that had opened up in Redondo Beach a few months earlier. Tiffani had chosen it for her first date because it was nice without being too fancy. The candlelit tables with their red-checked tablecloths were informal and romantic at the same time, and the stucco walls and pillars formed a series of private nooks.

She reached up to touch the red carnation she'd fixed in her hair with a comb. There were people sitting at several tables, but none of the guys she saw was wearing a carnation or seemed to be looking for anyone special.

"I don't think my date has shown up yet," Tiffani told the maître d'. "I'll wait for him at a table, I guess."

A few moments later, she was seated at a small table that was set into one of the alcoves. She opened the menu her waiter brought her, but she was too nervous to actually read it.

"What have I gotten myself into?" she murmured.

Here she was, waiting for a total stranger to show up. What if the guy was a complete jerk? What if he didn't like her? What if he never even showed up? It would be too embarrassing!

Calm down! she ordered herself. *You can't*

just jump up and run out of here. Everything will be fine.

Taking a deep breath, she glanced at the mural of an Italian landscape that decorated the nook. The gentle hillside, red-roofed cottages, and deep blue sea were so romantic looking that she felt a little better. This was an adventure, right?

For the last few days, she had been eyeing different guys in Sharkey's and at school, wondering which one of them would show up tonight. Any second now, she was finally going to find out! Was he going to be tall or short? Light-haired or—

"Tiffani?"

A boy's voice broke into Tiffani's thoughts. She felt an anxious flush rise to her cheeks as she turned to see who it was. Then she frowned and let out the breath she'd been holding.

"Sly? What are *you* doing here?" she asked. She glanced nervously in the direction of the restaurant entrance. "Listen, I don't want to be rude, but I'm waiting for someone, and I don't want him to get scared off by seeing another guy."

"I have a date, too," Sly said. His initial look of surprise melted into a grin. "In fact, I think—"

"Here?" Tiffani cut in, stifling a bubble of disappointment. Meeting a blind date was an uncomfortable enough situation *without* Sly hovering around. With him in the same restaurant, she doubted she would be able to relax at all.

Sly raised an eyebrow, giving her a cockeyed glance. "Um, Tiffani, don't you get it?"

"Get what?" she asked.

Why was he looking at her like that? Giving him a closer look, Tiffani saw that Sly had actually dressed up for his date. In his crisp, button-down shirt and pleated cotton pants, he looked pretty handsome, she had to admit. He was even wearing a jacket. "Sly, your date is really going to be impressed when she sees—"

Tiffani broke off as her gaze fell on Sly's lapel. She drew her breath in sharply. "Is that a carnation? A *red* carnation?" she asked, her mouth falling open.

Even before he nodded, Tiffani knew the answer, but somehow, she couldn't quite believe it. "You mean, *you're* my mystery date?"

"At your service," Sly said, making an exaggerated bow.

All she could do was stare at him in shock. One thought kept running through her mind: Her date was turning into a total disaster!

Jenny tapped her shoe impatiently against the rock and rubbed her arms.

Where is Sean? she wondered, glancing nervously around.

It had been a good half hour since the sun had

sunk below the horizon. Shadows now darkened the cove, and a cool breeze had whipped the surf into frothy whitecaps, sending a chill through her.

Why was he keeping her waiting this way?

"Sean?" Jenny called out tentatively. She peered into the inky blackness of the surrounding trees and rocks. Wind whistled through the leaves, but she couldn't see or hear anything that looked like a person.

"Are you out there, Sean?" she called again, more loudly this time. "This isn't funny, you know."

She waited for him to answer or appear, but he didn't. Finally, Jenny jumped down from the rock, kicking at the sand in frustration.

"This is just great," she muttered. "I've been stood up!"

"So what do you think, Tiffani? Are we made for each other, or what?" Sly asked. He broke off a piece of bread and spread some butter on it, then popped it into his mouth.

"If I have to choose between 'made for each other' and 'what,' I'll take 'what,'" Tiffani decided, laughing. "Don't take this personally, Sly, but I've never thought of you as boyfriend material, that's all. We know each other too well. It would be like dating my own brother."

Sly looked relieved to hear her say that. "I

know what you mean," he said. "I almost had a heart attack when I first saw that carnation in your hair." He held up his hands defensively. "How was I supposed to know that you're Blondie?"

"You should have listened to me when I told you not to answer that ad," Tiffani reproached him. "But I have to say, your answer to my ad was really great. If you wrote stuff like that in all your replies, I'm sure you'll have tons of dates."

"Thanks to you," Sly said. Giving her an impish smile, he explained, "You see, Tony told me about the advice you and Jenny gave him about what girls like to hear."

"No *wonder* I fell for it," Tiffani exclaimed, laughing. Shooting Sly a grin, she added, "Well, since we're stuck with each other, we might as well at least enjoy a nice dinner together."

"You said it," Sly agreed. He opened his menu and then looked at her over the top of it. "But since this isn't *really* a date, we'll go dutch, right?"

Tiffani rolled her eyes at him. "Don't ever change, Sly," she teased.

As he turned to signal for the waiter, Tiffani glanced around the restaurant again. Emilio's had gotten even more crowded since she'd arrived. Almost all of the tables were full now, and the sounds of voices and clanking dishes echoed off the walls.

"I'm glad we got here pretty early," she told Sly. "Otherwise we might not have gotten a ta—"

She gasped and broke off in the middle of the word as her gaze fell on a familiar face across the room. "I don't believe this!" she said, dropping her voice to an urgent whisper. "Sly, look over there!"

Sly looked. "Sean Flynn," he said, shrugging. "So?"

"So?" Tiffani rolled her eyes. "*So* he's supposed to be on a date with Jenny tonight!" She turned her head to get another look at the people Sean was sitting with—a middle-aged couple and . . . "And why is he with that girl again!"

Seeing the confused expression on Sly's face, Tiffani quickly told him about seeing Sean with the girl in the Corvette the week before.

When Tiffani was done, Sly glared darkly over at Sean's table. For a moment, she was afraid he might go over there and punch Sean or something. He *did* tend to get protective where Jenny was concerned.

"What a slime bucket! You mean, he's supposed to be out with Jenny, but instead he's with that girl again," he said darkly. "It even looks as if he's meeting her parents or something."

Tiffani nodded. "This is awful!" she exclaimed in a low voice. "What are we going to tell Jenny?!"

Chapter 8

Matt locked his car doors and gazed toward the entrance of the Redondo Beach Cineplex. The huge marquees on either side of the ticket windows announced the eight different movies being shown, but Matt wasn't really paying attention to the selections.

Reaching into his jeans pocket, he pulled out the page he'd ripped from *The Clarion* and reread the personal ad he'd circled: *Our happy ending will be better than anything in the movies. . . .*

Matt didn't pretend to understand what had been going through Randi Jo's mind these past few days. On the one hand, she'd written him this incredibly hopeful ad. And yet, every time he'd seen her during the week, she had acted cool and distant toward him. He couldn't help wondering whether she really wanted to work things out or not.

"There's only one way to find out," he told himself.

He jogged toward the entrance to the movie theater, feeling anxious and excited at the same time. He hadn't gotten dressed up, exactly, but he *had* worn his least ratty pair of jeans and a new striped shirt. It was almost as if he and Randi Jo were going out for the first time.

Matt slowed his pace as he drew closer to the entrance. His eyes searched over the long line of ticket holders and the knots of people waiting for friends, but he didn't catch sight of Randi Jo's tall figure or long blond hair. Apparently, she hadn't shown up yet.

Shoving his hands into his pockets, Matt walked to the edge of the crowd and stood a little apart, next to a poster advertising one of the movies. Maybe she had decided not to meet him after all, he thought. If she was really mad about his canceling their date earlier that week, she might have changed her mind about wanting a happy ending with him. . . .

"Matt?"

"Randi Jo?" Her name was already out of his mouth before he turned around and saw that it wasn't his girlfriend standing there.

"Chloe!"

Matt was surprised at how happy he was to see

her. He couldn't help noticing how cute Chloe looked in the T-shirt and flowered vest she had on with her jeans, or the way her dark eyes twinkled when she smiled at him.

But then he remembered why he had come to the movie theater in the first place. If Randi Jo saw him with Chloe, she was sure to get the wrong idea.

"So, uh, what movie are you seeing?" he asked, looking around uncomfortably.

Chloe laughed and lightly punched his arm. "Come on, Matt, stop kidding around," she told him. Crossing her arms over her vest, she gave him an appraising look. "I wasn't sure you'd show up tonight. I mean, after you didn't answer my first personal ad—"

"Personal ad?" Matt stared at Chloe, trying to make sense of what she was saying. "Are you saying that you *expected* to meet me?"

A glimmer of confusion came into Chloe's eyes. "Yeah. You mean, you *didn't* expect to meet me?"

His blank look must have answered her question. Shaking her head, she said, "What am I going to do with you, Matt? First you didn't even realize that my ad about the rock-and-roll renegade was meant for you. . . ."

"You wrote it for *me*?" Matt could hardly believe one of the cutest, most interesting girls at school had been flirting with him, and he hadn't even realized it. "I barely looked at the personals when they came out," he admitted. "But I sort of remember my friends talking about that one. Man, do *I* feel like an idiot."

"That's why I decided to give you a second chance." She frowned, letting out a sigh. "But it's pretty obvious that you were expecting someone else. Oh, well, so much for happy endings."

She started to turn away, but Matt grabbed her arm. "Happy endings . . . you wrote *that* ad, too!"

He slapped his palm against his forehead, realizing the mistake he'd made. How could he have been so blind! He'd been *sure* the ad was from Randi Jo. His mind raced as he went over the words in his head.

"So when you said I wasn't there for you last week, you were talking about not answering your first personal ad?" he guessed.

Chloe nodded. "Keen deduction, Sherlock," she said with a teasing grin.

"But what did you mean about working it out?" Matt asked. "I mean, we don't know each other that well. What could we possibly have to work out?"

"I was talking about getting the gig with the Rockets," she answered. "What did *you* think the ad meant?"

"I thought—"

Chloe put a hand over his mouth, cutting off his answer. "Never mind. Forget I asked. If you ask me, you do entirely too *much* thinking, Matt. You know what *I* think?"

"What?" he asked. Gazing down at her, he saw a dimple on her chin that he hadn't noticed before. Without thinking, he reached over to touch it.

"I think it's time we took a different approach to what's going on here—one that's not so . . . intellectual."

Matt wasn't sure who kissed whom first. But when their lips met, he gave in to the irresistible urge to wrap his arms tightly around Chloe. An electric charge shot through him like a bolt of lightning, and her sweet smell completely overwhelmed him.

"Hey!"

The sound of an angry, familiar voice barely broke into Matt's consciousness. It sounded muted, far away. Then he felt a hand push roughly into his back, and he realized that the person was right next to him.

Matt opened his eyes and took a woozy step back from Chloe. They were standing next to the exit, he realized, and a stream of people had started to emerge from the theater. Turning to face the person who had interrupted them, Matt said,

"What's the big idea? Can't you see I'm—"

He froze when he saw Randi Jo standing there. Angry spots of color reddened her cheeks, and there were tears in her eyes. Lowell and another guy were standing right behind her, looking very uncomfortable.

"How could you do this to me!" Randi Jo cried, blinking furiously.

Matt felt worse than he ever had in his life. "Randi Jo, I—"

"Don't insult me by trying to make excuses, Matt!" Her blue eyes darted accusingly back and forth between him and Chloe. "Couldn't you even be bothered to tell me to my face that you're breaking up with me? Is that how little you think of me?"

Tears were streaming down Randi Jo's cheeks now. Matt wanted to reach over to wipe them away, but he felt stuck, unable to say or do anything.

"*Oooh!* I hate you, Matt Garrison!" Randi Jo exclaimed. And she started to run off.

Matt opened his mouth to call after her, but no sound came out. All he could do was watch helplessly as Randi Jo ran out of his life.

By the time Matt got home and dragged himself up the stairs to his room, it was after ten o'clock. He had tried calling Randi Jo over a dozen times, stopping at every pay phone he passed on the drive back to his house. Each time, Randi Jo's mother had told him the same thing—Randi Jo didn't want to talk to him.

Not that he blamed her. Matt felt awful about what had happened. He was still trying to figure out for himself why he had kissed Chloe, and he hadn't come up with any answers that made any sense to him.

He was about to close the door to his room when he changed his mind and instead went across the hall to Jenny's room. In response to his tap on the door, she called out, "Come in."

As soon as he saw his sister slumped against her pillows, fiddling with the dial of her radio, Matt could tell that she had been crying. Her eyes were all red and puffy, and she looked sadder than he'd ever seen her.

"Hey, what's the matter?" Matt asked. He hurried over to sit on the edge of her bed, immediately forgetting about his own problems.

Jenny wiped her eyes and gave him a dejected look. "I had a really special date planned with Sean tonight, and he stood me up! Then Sly and Tiffani came by, and they were each other's blind dates, which would have been kind of funny except that I got totally depressed because they saw Sean with that girl again. Matt, I don't know what to think!"

Her words came out in such a confused jumble

that Matt wished he could replay it all at a slower speed. He didn't get what she meant about Tiffani and Sly's dates, but what he understood about Sean made Matt worry.

"Sean stood you up to go out with another girl?" he asked, frowning.

"It looks that way," Jenny replied. "The same one we saw him with in the car last week, remember?"

"In the red Corvette." Matt hadn't given the incident much thought since then—he'd had too much else on his mind. He wasn't sure what he could have done to change things, but he felt badly about not being more aware of the situation. "He didn't call to explain or *anything*?"

Jenny shook her head, plucking at her bedspread. "I tried to call *him* when I got home, but there wasn't any answer."

Seeing his sister so upset, Matt felt like driving over to Sean's house and punching the guy. "Sean's going to have some heavy-duty explaining to do the next time I see him!" he declared angrily. "How could he *do* this to you?"

"Hold it! I mean, thanks for being a macho big brother and all, but this is between Sean and me," Jenny said firmly. "If anyone's going to demand an explanation, it's going to be me!"

Matt was relieved to see some of the spunk

return to his sister's eyes. She even smiled. "I guess I've complained enough for one night," she told him. "How come *you're* so down?"

"Oh, no special reason. I just totally wrecked my relationship with Randi Jo, that's all," Matt said. He let out his breath in a frustrated rush and then told Jenny about what had happened at the theater.

"Wow! Randi Jo actually saw you *kissing* Chloe?" she said when he was done. Then she gave him a funny look. "Um, Matt, why *did* you kiss her? Didn't you tell me yourself that there's nothing romantic between you and Chloe?"

"I didn't *think* there was," he began, trying to work it out in his own mind. "I mean, I *love* Randi Jo. It's just that we've been fighting so much lately. . . . I'm not sure we have anything in common anymore. And then Chloe comes along, and she loves music and wants to do all the same kinds of things I do. . . ."

"Not to mention that she wants you to be her rock-and-roll renegade," Jenny put in, with a teasing smile.

Matt could feel the heat on his face. "When I saw her tonight, I thought she was the most adorable, vivacious girl I'd ever met. *That's* why I kissed her." He took a deep breath, letting it out slowly. "But I still really care about Randi Jo, too. It's hard to imagine *not* going out with her."

"Well, after tonight, you'd better get used to the idea," Jenny said. "Besides, you can't keep stringing Randi Jo along when you're obviously attracted to someone else. It isn't fair to her."

Matt knew his sister was right. "I guess it *is* kind of exciting to think that now I can get to know Chloe better," he said with a small smile.

He was definitely going to miss Randi Jo, but maybe it was time for a change. In his mind's eye, he pictured Chloe's petite figure, the special way she had looked at him outside the movie theater, and how nice it had felt to kiss her.

Yes, he was definitely going to enjoy getting to know her better.

Chapter 9

"**N**ate, have you seen Sean?"

Jenny stopped the tall, gangly boy in the hallway on her way to biology lab Monday morning. Not only was Nate Solar Energy's drummer, he also happened to be Sean's best friend. If anyone at Pacific Coast High knew where Sean was, it would be Nate.

Nate tucked his books under his arm and raked a hand through his wiry black hair. "I haven't seen him," he told her.

"Oh." Jenny couldn't help feeling dejected. She had hoped Sean would appear at her locker before the first bell, the way he usually did. When he hadn't, she'd gone to *his* locker, but he hadn't shown up there, either.

"It's not like him to pull a disappearing act like this," she said, talking more to herself than to Nate. "Where could he be?"

Nate shifted his weight from one foot to another, looking uneasily up and down the hall. "I, uh, guess maybe he's not in school," he mumbled.

"I don't get it," Jenny said, feeling more and more frustrated. "He's not at home—I already tried calling him there—and he didn't say a word to me about missing school. Are you sure he didn't say anything to you?"

Jenny thought she detected a glimmer of nervousness in Nate's eyes. "Um, not that I remember," he said. He took a few steps down the hall. "I've really got to get to class, Jenny. See you."

There was a sinking feeling in Jenny's stomach as she watched him walk away. *He sure was in a hurry to get away from me*, she thought. And he was definitely acting nervous. What did he know that she didn't?

All morning long, that question churned in her head. By the time she met her friends for lunch in the cafeteria, Jenny could only think of one answer.

"Sean is cutting school to be with *her*," she announced, plunking down her tray at the table where Tiffani, Tony, and Sly were already sitting.

Her friends broke off talking to look at her.

"Why do I have the feeling I missed part of this conversation?" Tony asked. "What are you talking about, Jenny?"

"The girl we saw Sean with in the Corvette?" Tiffani guessed, looking concerned.

Jenny nodded, sinking into a chair. "The same one you saw him having dinner with at Emilio's while I was waiting for him on some freezing rock," she added dejectedly. "I really feel like a fool. Can someone please tell me what I did to deserve this?"

"Nothing!" Tiffani said emphatically.

"The guy's a jerk, that's all," Sly added. "You didn't get to talk to him about what happened yet?"

Jenny shook her head. "Sean's not even in school, and his best friend just totally avoided me when I tried to find out where he is."

"I don't get it," Tiffani said, frowning. "It would be bad enough if he just came right out and said he wanted to break up with you. But if that's true, then why has he been so romantic lately? Why bother to ask you out on a dream date in the first place?"

"That's the ten-million-dollar question." Jenny groaned as the picture of Sean in the Corvette came back to her. "I wish I knew what was going on. How can I compete with some girl I've never even met?"

"Not to mention an older girl who looks really

hot," Tony put in, "and who might be more sophisticated, more worldly, more—"

"*Tony!*" Tiffani silenced him with a glare.

Tony shook himself. "Oh—what I meant to say is that Sean is obviously a deadbeat who's not good enough for you, Jenny. If you ask me, you should dump Sean and find a new boyfriend."

Sly grinned at her. "I'm available for that job, in case you didn't already know it. Just say the word."

"Thanks for the offer," she told him, smiling back. Even if this *was* the worst day in her life, it felt good to know that her friends were behind her 100 percent. "You guys are the best."

Still, as she ate her yogurt, Tony's description of the girl in the Corvette echoed in Jenny's mind. People had always told her that she was really together, very mature for her age. It was something Jenny had always been proud of. But now she couldn't help wondering if maybe Sean had found someone he liked more than her.

Just thinking about the possibility made her feel as if her heart would split right in two.

"I can't believe I'm standing in the same room as the Electric Swans," Matt said Monday night, bending down to speak into Chloe's ear.

He let his gaze roam around the hotel suite where the band was celebrating the release of their new album. Bright lights had been set up by the sofa, where the band's four members were posing for photographers, striking all kinds of wacky poses. The rest of the room was filled with people—everything from wild metalheads with leather jackets and ripped jeans to middle-aged executives with immaculate suits and striped ties. Matt had never seen such a varied crowd.

"A lot of bigwigs in the music scene are here tonight," Chloe said, her eyes skimming the crowd. "There's Quentin Cole, the head of Sigma Records. And that guy over there with the red leather top hat is—"

"Johnnie Lawless!" Matt exclaimed. "The VJ from MTV!"

Chloe nodded excitedly. "Something tells me this is going to be our lucky night," she predicted. "If the Rockets are going to show up anywhere, it'll be here."

"I hope you're right," Matt said, stifling a yawn.

"Hey, are you bored or something?" Chloe shot him a look of mock insult. "And here I thought I was showing you the time of your life."

"You are," Matt hurried to assure her. "It's just that we've been doing so much running around that I haven't had time for some other things—you know, like band practice, eating, and sleeping

. . . that sort of thing. My folks haven't exactly been crazy about my going out on so many school nights, either, but I don't have any regrets." He slipped an arm around her waist. "None at all, as a matter of fact."

The past week had been great. Chloe had taken him to every place she could think of in L.A. where the Rockets, their manager, or people from the Skydome might show up. Even though they hadn't met anyone associated with the band yet, Matt felt as if he was really becoming a part of one of the biggest music scenes in the country. Chloe had introduced him to more musicians, DJ's, and music journalists than he could keep track of.

"You know, it's amazing to be able to talk to so many people who are as nuts about music as I am," he told her. "It's too bad the rest of the band can't be here, too."

Chloe waved her hand dismissively. "They'll get over it. Besides, from what I've seen, *you're* the brains behind California Dreams. I think it's good for you to see the other music that's out there—the other possibilities. Who knows? Maybe you'll meet someone who could help you get into something . . . bigger."

For a second, Matt thought she meant leave California Dreams. But then he realized that couldn't be true. After all, Chloe was going out of her way to help the whole band by trying to get them the gig with the Rockets. She wouldn't do that if she were only interested in him.

"It would be great if the Dreams could get a gig in an L.A. club," he agreed. "I'm dying to play here somewhere." He reached an arm around the metallic tunic she wore with black velvet leggings. "I have to admit, ever since you've been taking me around places, I feel totally spoiled."

"If that's your way of saying thank you, you're welcome," Chloe said, grinning up at him.

"Actually, that's *not* my way of saying thank you. This is. . . ." He bent to give her a light, "thank you" sort of kiss, but somehow his lips lingered on hers.

"Ahem. *Excuse* me, you two lovebirds."

Matt straightened up and looked at the muscular black guy who had just spoken. He was wearing close-fitting black jeans, heavy leather boots, and a bright red leather vest with no shirt.

"Calvin! It's great to see you!" Chloe said, hugging him. "Calvin and I were both DJ's at my old high school," she explained to Matt.

"Cool." Matt shook hands with Calvin. "What kind of show did you do?"

"Rock, rap, a little heavy metal . . . I used to have a lot of local bands on."

Matt grinned at Chloe. "Chloe's been doing the same kind of thing at our school," he said.

"It's a great way to give bands some publicity," Calvin said. "More than they would get at some dinky school dance, anyway."

Matt felt himself grow defensive. There was something in Calvin's attitude that rubbed him the wrong way. California Dreams had played at some school dances, and Matt had always loved them. Other teenagers were their biggest fans, after all. It was fun to play for them. He flashed on all the hard work Randi Jo was putting into *The Clarion*'s dance. He didn't think she would appreciate someone calling the dance "dinky."

Hey, Calvin didn't mean anything by it, Matt told himself. After all, the music scene here in L.A. was a lot bigger than in Redondo Beach.

"Hey, why are you so quiet all of a sudden?" Chloe asked, after Calvin had walked away to get something to eat.

"It's nothing," Matt said. He didn't want to seem like some small-town rube. "I guess I'm just feeling guilty about not having time to help out Randi Jo with this weekend's dance."

Chloe rolled her eyes. "I don't see what the big deal is," she said. "You guys have broken up. It's not like you owe her anything."

"I did promise," he said.

"This is much more important," she said adamantly. "If you really want to be a success, the band has to come first. California Dreams is never going to get any *big* gigs if you spend all your time making decorations and stuff."

Looking at the growing crowd of people filling up the hotel suite, Matt had to admit that Chloe had a point. This was definitely the place to be for a musician on the way up. Maybe it *was* dumb to feel guilty about not helping with the dance.

Matt smiled at Chloe, hoping to shake the moody cloud that had fallen over him. "So, do you see anyone who might be able to help us get an in with the Rockets?"

As Chloe bubbled on about someone she wanted to introduce him to, Matt tried to envision California Dreams' future success. But the only picture he could conjure up was Randi Jo's hurt and disappointed face.

Chapter 10

Tony cocked his head to one side and surveyed the piece of poster board he'd been working on. Taking the paintbrush from the container of red poster paint, he gave a few final strokes and then stood back to look again.

"That is truly hot," he decided. "A Tony Wicks original." He picked it up and held it out for Jenny, Tiffani, and Sly to see. "It could be worth millions after I become famous."

His friends were bent over the gym floor, working on their own posters. Glancing up at his design, Jenny said, "I'm sure Randi Jo will be eternally grateful that you're letting your famous . . . um . . ." She broke off, peering at Tony's poster board more closely. "What's it supposed to be, anyway?" she asked.

"Lightning bolts!" he said, glaring at her. "Can't you tell? I want to send everyone the message that Saturday night's dance is going to be charged!"

Getting to his feet, Sly took the poster from Tony and turned it upside down and then turned it upside down again. "Which way does it go?" he asked.

Tony grabbed the poster back and glared at Sly. "I should have known *you* wouldn't appreciate my talent. Hey, Randi Jo!" he called as she passed by. "Check this out."

Randi Jo paused, holding a bottle of glue in one hand and some plastic containers of sprinkles in the other. "Hi, you guys. Your posters are great," she said, gesturing to the line of them on the gym floor. "Once we put them up for Saturday's dance, this place will look fantastic."

She smiled as she spoke, but Tony thought her face seemed a little strained. It had to be awkward for her, being with all of her ex-boyfriend's closest buddies.

"Thanks for helping out after . . ." Randi Jo's smile faded, and she gave an uneasy wave. "Well, you know."

"Just because you and Matt aren't going out anymore doesn't mean that we can't be friends," Jenny said.

"Anyway, we promised we'd help," Tiffani

pointed out. "We're not about to go back on our word or anything."

The way Matt did, Tony added to himself. He hadn't given the situation a lot of thought until right now, but he was beginning to get the feeling that Randi Jo had gotten shortchanged by Matt. Not only was he dating another girl, he hadn't done any of the things he'd promised to help Randi Jo with for Saturday's dance.

"Thanks, you guys. That means a lot to me." Randi Jo started to say something else but was interrupted as Lowell came up to her.

"Marcia needs those sparkles," he told Randi Jo. "And we need to decide where the band's going to set up so we can decorate that area. . . ."

"I feel like a real jerk," Jenny said as Lowell led Randi Jo toward the other end of the gym. "It wasn't exactly great of us to back out of playing at Saturday's dance."

"I know what you mean," Tiffani agreed. "And Randi Jo is being so nice about it that I feel even worse. If I were her, I'd be pretty mad at us for being so self-involved."

Sly held up a hand. "Wait a minute. It was a choice between playing for a high school dance or playing with the Rockets!" he said. "I mean, I feel bad for Randi Jo, too, but I still say we were doing what was best for the band."

"But we totally let down a good friend when

she really needed our support," Jenny said thoughtfully. "I'm not sure it was worth it."

Tony took a fresh piece of poster board and set it down on the gym floor. "Besides which, Matt and Chloe haven't had any more luck than you did in getting us to play with the Rockets, Sly. *And* he missed rehearsal yesterday and the day before."

"Chloe has had something he absolutely *has* to do every single day," Tiffani said. "Maybe I'm just jealous that none of the rest of us ever get to go along, but . . ." She shot a questioning glance at the others and asked, "Does anyone besides me have the feeling that Chloe doesn't want Matt to spend much time with the rest of us?"

"Yo, don't forget that we *all* decided that they should try to get us the gig with the Rockets," Tony pointed out. "But it *does* seem weird that suddenly Matt doesn't have a single second for the band. I mean, even if they *do* get us hooked up with the Rockets, we'll sound terrible if we haven't rehearsed."

"Maybe we need to convince Matt to slow down a little so that the band doesn't forget how to play. I'll try to talk to him," Jenny promised.

Letting out a deep sigh, she added, "This is great. My brother *and* my boyfriend are both acting as if aliens have taken control of their brains."

Tony had been thinking so much about Matt and California Dreams that he'd completely forgotten about Jenny's boy problems. "Sean still pulling that disappearing act?" he asked.

Jenny nodded. "He hasn't been in school all week," she said quietly. "I'd rather not talk about it, if you don't mind."

Tony decided not to mention that *she'd* been the one to bring up Sean in the first place. He looked at Sly, who shrugged and said, "Sure. Okay. So let's talk about *my* love life."

"That ought to take about thirty seconds, since all the girls around here with any sense are dating *me*," Tony put in.

"Will you guys stop this macho competition over every girl you see?" Tiffani said, rolling her eyes. "Considering all the ads in the personals, I'm sure *both* of you are getting tons of dates."

Sly didn't appear to have heard her, though. Shooting Tony a smug look, he said, "For your information, big shot, I've already been out with three girls. Not including you, Tiffani," he added quickly, "since that wasn't a *real* date."

"Gee, thanks," Tiffani told him.

"Well, I've been out with three girls, too," Tony shot back. "And I've got another date for tonight."

"What are you going to do?" Jenny asked.

"We're having dinner at Emilio's," Tony replied. "That reminds me, I have to go out and get a carnation, so my date will recognize me."

"Oh, no!" Tiffani said in a horrified whisper. "I don't believe it's happening again!"

"*What*'s happening again?" Tony asked. He saw that Tiffani's face had gone completely white, but for some reason, Sly had started cracking up. "What's going on?" he demanded.

Sly gasped for breath, trying to stop laughing. He pointed at Tiffani and said, "Tony . . . I'd like you to meet your date . . . Blondie."

Tony stared blankly at Tiffani. "You?"

She nodded. "How come I keep getting dates with people I already know?" she said, throwing up her hands. "That's it—I'm giving up on these personals. They're a total failure."

"I don't know about that," Tony said, thinking about it. "I think they *sort* of work, anyway."

"How do you figure that?" Jenny asked, shooting him a dubious glance. "I mean, have any of you met a guy or girl you'd want to date?"

"Not yet," Sly admitted.

He stared at Tony, who shrugged and said, "Me, neither. But we did all got hooked up with people we really get along well with. . . ."

"One another!" Tiffani finished, grinning at him. "I guess you're right. I won't give up completely on the personals until after my next date," she decided. "I just hope it doesn't turn out to be with Matt!"

● ● ●

Thursday morning, Jenny closed her locker and started making her way toward homeroom. When she realized that she'd automatically started to take the long way—the route that just happened to lead her past Sean's locker—she frowned and stopped.

"Why torture yourself?" she murmured. "He's not going to be there."

All week long, she'd found excuses to pass by Sean's locker. He hadn't shown up Monday, Tuesday, or Wednesday. There was no reason to think that today would be any different. Jenny had called his house more times than she could count, but no one ever answered. And if Nate knew anything about where Sean was, he wasn't about to fill her in. He practically ran the other way every time he saw her.

Jenny let out a deep sigh and shifted her books from one arm to the other. It was bad enough that Sean was probably going out with another girl. What was really infuriating was that she had no way to find out for sure. Until she did, Jenny knew it would be impossible to even *start* getting over Sean and to get on with her life. It was almost as if she were in some weird science-fiction movie where she was stuck in a nightmarish limbo.

She blinked as someone bumped into her. She'd been so lost in thought that she hadn't even been aware that she'd started walking again. In three more steps, she would round the next corner and Sean's locker would come into sight.

You idiot, she thought to herself. Still, she couldn't seem to stop herself from taking those three steps. As she rounded the corner, her eyes moved automatically to her boyfriend's locker, about ten feet away—and she stopped dead in her tracks.

"I don't believe you're here!" she exclaimed, gaping at Sean. She closed her eyes and counted to five, but when she opened them again, he was still there. This time, she wasn't about to let him get away!

Squaring her shoulders, Jenny stormed over to Sean. "Where have you been?" she demanded.

"Jenny!" Sean's eyes lit up when he saw her, but Jenny wasn't about to fall for his romantic act again.

"No games, Sean. I want to know what's going on. Why did you stand me up last Saturday? And why haven't you been in school all week?" She crossed her arms over her chest and waited, tapping her foot on the corridor floor.

Sean looked down, and a frown darkened his face. He pulled a few books from his locker before he could look at her again. "Jenny, this is really hard to say," he began.

Here it comes, Jenny thought. *He's about to tell me about the other girl.* Suddenly, she just wanted this whole scene over and done with.

"Look, you don't have to treat me like a charity case," she said angrily. "Why don't you just say it? You met someone new and you want to break up!"

"What . . .?" Sean was looking at her as if she'd gone totally crazy. "Jenny, what makes you think I met another girl?"

"Oh, come on," Jenny told him, growing more and more frustrated. "Do I have to spell it out for you? First, I see you in that red Corvette with a gorgeous girl you're obviously having a great time with. Second, you stand me up for the biggest date of my life, and on the same night, Tiffani and Sly happen to see you with that girl in Emilio's. Third, you disappear off the face of the planet, and your best friend treats me like I have a bad skin rash or something. . . ."

Jenny spoke in a rush, counting off the reasons on her fingers. Each time she ticked off another piece of evidence, Sean's face grew whiter and the look in his eyes grew more and more panicked.

"And fourth, you're acting totally guilty right now!" Jenny went on. She had kept her feelings bottled up all week, but now everything came pouring out. "Which makes me think that you've been cutting school to be with . . . whoever she is. I can't believe you pretended to still care about me. Were you *ever* planning on telling me about her?"

Sean's face fell. "You saw us together? Jenny, I didn't want you to know—"

"I'll bet you didn't! But I *do* know, and I'm not going to play the fool anymore!"

Suddenly Jenny didn't even know why she was bothering to talk to him about this. He'd as much as admitted that she was right about the other girl.

She whirled around to leave, but Sean grabbed her arm. "Jenny, wait! You've got it all wrong!"

"Tell me about it," she scoffed. Kids nearby had stopped to stare at them, but Jenny was too angry to care. "Are you trying to say that I just *imagined* I saw you with that girl?"

"No," he admitted. "But she's not a new girl-friend or anything. She's a real estate agent. My parents are selling our house, but they were out of town, so I had to be around when the agent showed the house to prospective buyers."

"You're not dating her? She's helping to sell your house?" Jenny tried to make sense of what he was telling her, but somehow, the two things he'd said didn't seem to go together at all. "But why?"

Sean stuffed his hands into his pockets. "This is what's so hard to tell you." He looked searchingly into her eyes. "I've known for a while, but I've been putting off saying anything. . . ."

He was so serious that Jenny knew it had to be

something awful. "What?" she asked urgently. "What is it?"

"My dad's company is transferring him to San Francisco," Sean explained. "We're moving there in a couple of weeks."

Chapter 11

"**A** couple of weeks!" Jenny's mouth fell open, and she stared at Sean in dismay. She couldn't believe he was moving away from Redondo Beach—away from *her*.

"Wow . . . I mean, I'm glad you're not dating someone else, but . . ." She let out her breath in a rush. "You're really leaving? So soon?"

He nodded, barely able to look her in the eye. "Everything I care about is here. My band, my friends . . . I'm really going to miss being here. But most of all, I'm going to miss *you*, Jenny."

Jenny blinked back the tears that came to her eyes. Suddenly a million questions came to mind. "Why did you wait until now to tell me?" she asked. "Why did you let me think you wanted to break up with me? Why did you ask me to think up my dream date if you were going to stand me up like that?"

"I felt awful about that," Sean said apologetically. "I was just about to go meet you when Karen Duane called—she's the real estate agent. Anyway, she had a couple with her who wanted to see the house a second time. My parents were in San Francisco looking for a place for us to live there, so I had to be available to show our house *here* to prospective buyers. I tried to put Karen off, but she was really pushy. And when I called your house—"

"You called?" Jenny interrupted. "But I never got the message!"

Now Sean was the one who looked surprised. "Dennis said you'd already left, but I made him promise to tell you how sorry I was that I couldn't make it."

"Dennis? No *wonder* I didn't get your message. Ten-year-old boys aren't the most reliable when it comes to that kind of thing."

Jenny was starting to get a clearer picture of what had happened, but there were still a few things that didn't make sense to her. "What about Tiffani and Sly seeing you at Emilio's?" she asked, frowning. "And how come you've been avoiding me all week?"

"Let me finish explaining," Sean insisted. "Anyway, I guess staying behind to show that couple the house was worth it, because they decided to buy it. . . ."

"Congratulations," Jenny said bleakly.

Sean frowned at her. "Believe me, I feel exactly the same way. But everyone else was so psyched about the deal that they all decided to go out to dinner, and they insisted that I go with them."

"And *that's* why you were at Emilio's," Jenny realized. She couldn't believe how twisted around everything had gotten.

"Yup. And I didn't just disappear, either," Sean explained. "My folks called after I got home that night. They decided to buy a co-op instead of a house, and the co-op board wanted to meet the whole family—"

"Including the Flynn's brilliant, talented son, Sean?" Jenny guessed.

Sean flashed her a wry smile. "You got it. I flew to San Francisco Sunday morning, and then we stayed on a few extra days to register in a new school and get a feeling for the place."

He held up his hands, giving her a beseeching look. "That's the whole story, I swear. I'm sorry I didn't tell you sooner, but . . . well, I wanted to make the rest of our time together really special, and I thought that if you knew the truth, it would be too depressing." He let out a deep sigh. "I guess I really screwed up, huh?"

Jenny tried to act stern, but she didn't have it in her heart to be too hard on Sean. "I wish you'd told me the truth," she said, "but I *suppose* I can forgive you. At least you're not going out with someone else."

"No way." Sean took both of her hands and looked intently into her eyes. "There's no way I'd ever do that"—his voice dropped to a husky whisper—"not when I've got you."

When he bent to kiss her, Jenny didn't even care that they were right in the middle of the corridor, with kids all around them. The familiar tingle of excitement rushed through her from head to toe, but it didn't completely erase how sad she felt.

Don't think about the fact that he's moving away, she told herself. *Don't think about the fact that you don't know when you'll ever see him again!*

Matt was whistling to himself as he came in the kitchen door Thursday night. The band he and Chloe had gone to see that night had been really good—sort of a mix between rock and roll and reggae. Hearing them had given Matt an idea for a new song, and he couldn't wait to start working on it.

"Hi, Mom. Hi, Dad," he greeted his parents as he breezed through the living room.

Mr. Garrison glanced at his watch and then

frowned at Matt. "It's almost midnight. That's a little late to be out on a school night, don't you think?"

"It's never too late for a rock and roller who's on the move." Matt grinned, but the look on his dad's face told him that he wasn't amused. "Um, I'll still be able to catch plenty of Zs tonight," he added, more seriously.

"Well, I guess a few late nights are all right," his mother put in, "as long as you still get your homework done."

Matt smiled uneasily, trying not to think about the trigonometry homework that lay undone on his desk. "Mmm," he said noncommittally. "Well, um, g'night."

Before they could ask any more questions, he headed for the stairs, taking them two at a time. Usually, his parents were very laid back and understanding, but lately they seemed worried about how busy he'd been.

Maybe he *had* been out a little late on a few school nights, but if that was what it took to get an in with the Rockets, he was willing to make the sacrifice. So far, Chloe hadn't made the connections she'd hoped for, but she *did* know a lot of people in the music business. Matt was confident that one of her connections would pay off.

As he passed the open door to his sister's

room, Matt saw that Jenny was still awake, sitting at her desk in an oversize red nightshirt.

"You should have seen the band Chloe and I saw tonight," he said, leaning against her doorframe. "King Cobra—they were awesome!"

Jenny turned around at her desk, eyeing him with a look Matt didn't quite understand. "That's great, Matt. Is that why you missed rehearsal, because you went to see some band?"

Matt frowned at her sarcastic tone. "Do you have a problem with that?" he asked, crossing his arms over his chest. "The band agreed that Chloe and I should try to get us the gig as the Rockets' opening act. I can't help it if doing that means missing rehearsal once in a while."

"Once in a while?" Jenny shot him a dubious glance. "Matt, you haven't played with the Dreams a single time this week!"

"It's only temporary," Matt insisted. He shifted his weight to his other foot, growing more and more frustrated. "First Mom and Dad, and now you. Why is everyone getting on my case, anyway?"

Jenny looked at him for a moment before asking, "Did you and Chloe have any luck getting us to open for the Rockets?"

"Not yet. We've made a lot of connections, though, and Chloe's working on it."

"Matt, she's *been* working on it for over a

week," Jenny said, frowning over at him. "Don't you think it's time you admit that we're not going to be playing with them?"

"We don't know that for sure," he said.

"Well, I *do* know one thing for sure," Jenny countered. "Chloe has been usurping so much of your time that you've been neglecting the band *and* your friends. . . ."

Matt opened his mouth to object, but she held up a hand to stop him. "I know, I know . . . we *all* agreed to try this. All I'm saying is that it's time to give up. And even if we *did* decide to try to play with the Rockets, I don't think that justifies totally dropping all of your friends."

"I *haven't* dropped my friends!" Matt insisted. "What I'm doing is good for all of us! If you can't see that, then—"

Matt was interrupted by the shrill ringing of the upstairs phone. Still feeling frustrated, he strode out into the hall and picked up the receiver. "Hello?"

"Hi. I know it's late, but is, um, Jenny there?"

"Randi Jo?" Matt was sure he recognized her voice, but her tone was cool and distant. "Is that you?"

There was a short pause before she answered. "Yes. I'd like to speak with *Jenny*, please."

She must have recognized his voice, too, but she was treating him as if he were a total stranger. Matt let out a sigh, feeling his mood sink even more.

"It's for you, Jenny," he muttered, and held the phone out to her.

Why was everything such a mess? A week ago, *he* would have been the one Randi Jo would want to talk to. Now she didn't want to have anything to do with him, and his friends were all treating him as if he were some kind of criminal.

"Oh, my gosh! That's awful! What are you going to do?" Jenny's voice broke into Matt's thoughts, and he saw that she looked really concerned.

Matt wanted to ask what the matter was, but he stopped himself. *It's none of your business*, he reminded himself. He knew he didn't have a claim on Randi Jo or anything, but knowing that she had called Jenny, and not him, made him feel really weird.

Turning away, he went into his room, closed the door, and flicked on the radio. It was now after twelve-thirty, but he was too preoccupied to go to bed. Sitting down at his desk, he flipped open his trig book. "Might as well do something productive," he muttered.

He had only finished a few problems when a knock sounded on his door and Jenny came in.

"I hope you're satisfied, Matt," she said, shooting him an accusing stare.

"What did I do this time? Is it suddenly against the law for me to breathe? I feel as if I can't do *anything* right anymore!"

Jenny rolled her eyes. "If you'd stop feeling sorry for yourself, you might be able to see that we've caused Randi Jo a lot of trouble."

Hearing her name brought back the pangs of guilt that had been nagging at him whenever he thought of Randi Jo. "What happened?"

"The band Randi Jo got to replace the Dreams just canceled. The drummer's got the flu or something," Jenny explained. "The dance is the day after tomorrow, and Randi Jo doesn't have any idea who she can get to play."

Matt dropped his gaze, plucking at the edge of his trigonometry book. He couldn't stand the probing way Jenny was looking at him. It made him feel guiltier than ever.

"You and I both know that if we'd kept our promise to her, the Dreams would be playing on Saturday and Randi Jo wouldn't be in this mess," Jenny went on. "I told her I'd call Sean to see if Solar Energy can play, but—"

"That's a good idea," Matt put in quickly. But when he glanced up at Jenny, her frown told him that she didn't agree.

"Can't you even admit that we've been unfair?'' she asked, planting her hands on her hips. "It was really selfish of us to back out of doing the dance. . . ."

Matt opened his mouth, but before he could get a word out, Jenny said, "I'm not saying it's *your* fault. We're all guilty. I mean, I want to play with the Rockets as much as you do, but it shouldn't happen at the expense of a good friend."

"If we really care about the band, our music has to come first," Matt objected, but somehow the words didn't sound as convincing as when Chloe had said them to him earlier. "Anyway, it's a little late to do anything about it now, isn't it?"

"Not necessarily." Jenny faced him with a frank stare. "I could call Randi Jo back right now and tell her the Dreams will play."

Matt wasn't sure what to do. He *did* feel partly responsible for Randi Jo's predicament, but it was hard to just give up on getting the gig with the Rockets.

"If you wanted to make me feel like a complete worm, you've succeeded," he said, letting out a sigh. "But I don't know if the solution is as simple as you're making it sound, Jenny. I have to talk to Chloe first."

"What for?" Jenny asked. "This is something for the Dreams to decide. It doesn't have anything to do with Chloe."

"She said she was going to call some people

after she got home," Matt said. "What if she actually got us the opening spot for the Rockets? We couldn't just back out, not after all the trouble she's gone to."

Jenny looked as if she were going to object, but then she seemed to change her mind. "Okay," she finally relented. "But you have to promise to talk to her tomorrow. If she *hasn't* gotten us the gig, then we'll definitely play at Saturday's dance."

"Okay, it's a deal," Matt agreed.

The more he thought about it, the more he realized that playing *The Clarion*'s dance was the right thing to do. Even if he and Randi Jo weren't dating each other anymore, he still wanted to help out.

After Jenny said good night, Matt got into bed and tried to sleep, but his mind was racing. He wasn't sure why, but he kept thinking of Randi Jo—of her smile and the way she used to tease him about being obsessed with music. How had they gotten to be such enemies?

We don't have anything in common anymore, he reminded himself. *And I have everything in common with Chloe.*

The past week and a half had been the most exhilarating time of his life, and it was thanks to Chloe. He had never met anyone he could share music with the way he could share it with her. And she was definitely cute.

Then why did he keep thinking about Randi Jo?

Matt sighed, staring up at his darkened ceiling. He had hoped that breaking up with Randi Jo would help him make sense of his feelings, but he was more confused than ever.

Chapter 12

Matt yawned and stared bleary eyed at all the students who bustled past him in the hall at Pacific Coast High. Was it his imagination, or was school starting earlier and earlier these days?

He glanced at his watch. It was ten after eight—about the same time he got there every day. Everyone else looked awake enough. Why did *he* feel so tired?

"Maybe because you couldn't get to sleep until after three in the morning," he said aloud, answering his own question.

His mind had been swimming ever since his talk with Jenny the night before. He'd been so caught up with the L.A. music scene—and Chloe— that he hadn't really let himself think about how insensitive he'd been to Randi Jo. Now he realized that, even though they had broken up, he still wanted to be there for her as a friend.

Playing tomorrow night's dance would be a good way to show her that he still cared. But before he could commit himself to the gig, he had to talk to Chloe. The bell for homeroom wouldn't ring for another fifteen minutes or so—maybe he could catch up with her at KPCH before then.

When he opened the door to the radio station a few minutes later, Matt was glad to see that Chloe was there. She was sitting sideways in the upholstered chair in the outer room, her legs hooked over the chair arm. She was humming a tune to herself as she looked over a sheet of paper, swinging her feet in time to the music.

"Hi," Matt greeted her. "How come you look so awake, when I feel as if I've been stricken with African sleeping sickness or something?" He couldn't believe how alert she was—even the flowered minidress she wore seemed full of life.

Chloe grinned up at him. "I always feel energized after a night out with a cute guy." She waved the paper she was holding at him. "Plus, I'm just making up the list for my next show, and I started getting excited about the music."

"I know what you mean," Matt told her. He was about to tell her that it was like that for him whenever he worked on a song for the Dreams, but then he stopped himself. That wasn't why he'd come here, after all.

"So what brings you to KPCH?" Chloe asked, as if she could read his mind. "You missed me so much that you couldn't wait until we got together later on?"

She reached out to tweak the sleeve of his shirt, but Matt suddenly felt more uncomfortable than flattered. It was too . . . weird to be flirting with Chloe when he had to talk to her about Randi Jo.

"Actually, I was wondering if you had any luck getting us an in with the Rockets," Matt said. "Because if you didn't—"

"Oh—you're going to die when you hear this!" Chloe cut in excitedly. "When I got home last night, there was a message from a friend of mine who knows someone on the Rockets' road crew. . . ."

That didn't sound like someone who had a lot of clout, but Matt still felt a buzz of excitement. "So, are we going to open for the Rockets? I mean, the first show's tomorrow night. Isn't this cutting it kind of close?"

"My friend thinks we might be able to work something out," Chloe said. "Either for tomorrow's show or maybe for next week. I figured that you and I could meet up with him tonight at—"

"Hold it," Matt interrupted, holding up a hand. He couldn't let this go any further. "I'm giving up, Chloe. I want to stop trying to get us booked as the Rockets' opening band."

"What?" Chloe asked, raising a questioning brow. "You can't stop trying now that we're so close."

"Believe me, I don't want to, but"—Matt took a deep breath before continuing—"but Randi Jo's in trouble and I owe it to her to help her out."

He went on to tell her about the band that had backed out of playing for Saturday night's party. "I feel partly responsible, since we went back on our promise to play, too," Matt finished. "So the rest of the band and I have decided to do the dance after all."

Chloe was looking at him as if he were speaking some language she had never heard before. Then, shaking herself, she punched him lightly on the arm. "For a second there, I thought you were serious," she told him, laughing. "As if you'd really give up a chance to open for the Rockets. . . . Pretty funny, Matt."

"Chloe, I *am* serious," Matt said, frowning. "I can't just ignore my friends when they need me."

"What about the things *you* need? Aren't they important, too?" Chloe countered. "Opening for the Rockets could be the most important thing that's ever happened to you."

Matt tried not to think about that. "Well, it's been over a week and we haven't gotten the gig yet," he pointed out. "But it's not just that. I've been totally ignoring my friends *and* the band this past week. I mean, I've been having a great time with you, but I can't ignore my other responsibilities anymore."

"But, Matt, all that stuff is really small-time," Chloe said impatiently, jumping up from her chair. "Playing for Randi Jo's little dance can't be as important as getting a gig with the Rockets. And as for California Dreams"—she hesitated slightly before continuing—"can't they see that you guys will all benefit from the connections you're making? I mean, maybe they're holding you back. Maybe you should think about dropping them and hooking up with a better band."

Matt couldn't believe what he was hearing. "I could never just *drop* Jenny and Tiffani and Tony. They're my best friends, *and* they're great musicians," he said defensively.

Chloe shrugged. "I'm just trying to say that you might have a better shot at success if you hook up with other people who already have a little exposure. The only way you're going to get ahead is if you think about yourself first. If you don't realize that, you're being a fool."

Suddenly everything became clear to him— why Chloe didn't ever want the other California

Dreams to go with them, why she had been so dismissive about Randi Jo.

"I guess I *have* been a fool," he said slowly. "I thought you liked me the way I am, but that's not true, is it? You won't really be happy with me until I drop everything else in my life and become part of a successful L.A. band."

"There's nothing wrong with success, Matt," Chloe shot back.

Matt felt as if he were getting a glimpse of the real Chloe for the first time, and he didn't like what he saw at all. "There is, if it means letting you monopolize my life. There is, if it means alienating my friends," he told her.

"You'd make new friends," Chloe said, shrugging. "Friends you have more in common with. You have to admit, you *wanted* to meet people in the L.A. music scene. You've been totally into all the stuff we've been doing."

"Yeah, but it's not worth ruining everything else in my life for," he told her. "Maybe I haven't been acting as if I believe that, but I do."

For a moment, Chloe simply gazed back at him. "Music is my whole life, Matt," she finally said. "It comes before everything else. I don't think there's anything wrong with that." Giving an off-handed shrug, she added, "If you don't feel the same way, well, I don't think there's any point in our spending more time together."

"That's fine with me," Matt said automatically.

He couldn't believe how easily the words came out of his mouth. For the past week, he'd been sure that Chloe was the best thing that had ever happened to him. But now he didn't feel the least bit sad that they wouldn't be dating anymore.

"Well, I guess I'd better go," he said, shifting his books from one arm to the other. "See you."

Chloe turned back to the paper she'd been looking at. "Bye."

As Matt headed toward homeroom, he felt as if someone had lifted a twenty-ton weight from his shoulders. He couldn't wait to tell Tiffani, Jenny, Tony, and Sly the good news—that they would be able to play for *The Clarion*'s party after all. He was looking forward to spending more time with his *real* friends.

"Wish me luck, Jenny." Tiffani crossed her fingers as the two girls left Pacific Coast High after school.

"You don't need any luck," Jenny assured her. "I bet this date will be great. At least you know it can't be *worse* than being set up with Sly and Tony."

Tiffani giggled, rolling her eyes. "That's for sure." Patting the in-line roller skates that hung over her shoulder, she added, "This time I arranged an after-school date—we're going Roller Blading in the park. I figure that even if I don't like the guy, I'll at least have a good time skating."

"Smart planning," Jenny agreed. "Listen, I'm meeting Matt, Sly, and Tony at Sharkey's now to talk about tomorrow's dance. I'll call you later and let you know whether we're playing."

A worried look came into Tiffani's eyes. "What happens if Matt won't agree to it? What will Randi Jo do then?"

"I worked it all out with Sean," Jenny told her. "If the Dreams don't play, Solar Energy will. Either way, the dance will be fun."

"Still, I hope *we're* the ones who play," Tiffani put in. "That would show Randi Jo that we still care about her. Besides, we haven't had a gig in a while. It would be great if we could get things moving for the band again."

"No kidding," Jenny agreed with a nod. "It's funny—Matt and Chloe's plan was supposed to be good for the Dreams, but so far, all it's done is keep us *away* from our music."

"I just hope Matt decides to make the band a priority again now," Tiffani said. "Well, see you later, Jenny."

"Bye. And good luck!"

Tiffani gave a cheerful wave as Jenny walked off. Then she sat on the steps in front of the school entrance to put on her Roller Blades. That morning, she'd picked out her outfit carefully, wanting something comfortable that wouldn't restrict her movements. Glancing down at her white leggings and oversize pink T-shirt, she decided that her choice had been a good one. Somehow, dressing casually made her feel more comfortable about meeting her mystery date.

Once her skates were securely fastened and her kneepads on, Tiffani pulled her blond hair off her face with a pink stretchy headband. Then she placed her sneakers in her backpack, slipped it on, and pushed off toward Rollins Park.

The trip was a short one on skates. Within ten minutes, she was gliding toward the tree-lined paths where dozens of people were walking and skating around. A thick knot of pigeons gathered around an old man with bread crumbs, and Tiffani skated around them, heading for the sculpted stone fountain of three dolphins pulling the god Neptune.

Her gaze immediately searched out the bench closest to the three dolphins. That was where she had arranged to meet her date. Someone was sitting there, all right, but she didn't think he was her date. He just *couldn't* be.

Tiffani skated to a halt about ten feet away from the man, frowning. This guy had thinning gray hair and was wearing a suit that looked at least fifty years old. It had definitely been a long, long time since he had been in high school.

"Don't panic. My real date must be around here somewhere," she cautioned herself, swiveling her head around to search the area.

Suddenly a loud crash made her turn to her left. About a dozen feet away, a blond guy lay sprawled on the pavement, rubbing one of his legs just above the kneepad.

"Are you all right?" Tiffani asked, skating over to him. As she reached him, the guy looked over at her, and she realized she knew him from school. "You're Randi Jo's friend. Lowell, right?"

Lowell nodded and pushed himself up to a sitting position. "I recognize you, too. Tiffani— from California Dreams. I guess I'm okay. It's just that I've never been on Roller Blades before. The only reason I'm wearing them now is that I'm supposed to meet. . . ."

His voice trailed off, and he looked at Tiffani in surprise. "You?" he asked, pushing his glasses back up on his nose. "Are you Blondie?"

"Guilty," Tiffani told him. "And I guess you're my date."

She wasn't sure what to think. If she'd had to draw a picture of her ideal dream guy, it probably wouldn't have been Lowell. He did have nice eyes, she realized, the kind that seemed to change color every time he looked in a different direction. But he seemed a little . . . nerdy.

As soon as the thought crossed her mind, Tiffani felt guilty. *You just met the guy. You could at least give him a chance,* she told herself.

"Um, we could just sit and talk for a while if you don't feel like skating yet," she suggested.

Lowell looked grateful for the suggestion. Taking his elbow, Tiffani helped him to his feet, and they made their way to the nearest empty bench.

"You must be psyched about tomorrow night's dance," Tiffani began, trying to think of something to say.

"Yeah. I think a lot of people are going to show up," Lowell told her. "I just hope we get this whole band situation cleared up."

Tiffani shot him a guilty smile. "I feel really badly about the way we backed out," she told him. "But, actually, it looks as if the Dreams might be able to play after all. The rest of the band is deciding right now, as a matter of fact."

"Better late than never, I suppose," Lowell said with a shrug. "I was starting to think I'd have to call my dad and see what he could come up with."

"Your dad? How could he help?"

"He knows some people in the music business," Lowell explained. "I'd rather use a local band, but if that doesn't work out, he might be able to call in some favors and get someone else at the last minute."

"Your dad's into music? You mean, rock and roll and stuff?" Tiffani asked.

Lowell nodded. "I'm pretty lucky. Dad is one of the owners of the Skydome, so I get to see a lot of bands there. I just saw Nirvana play last month."

"I love them!" Tiffani exclaimed, looking at Lowell with new interest. Obviously, there was more to him than met the eye. "Who else have you—"

She broke off as something else he'd said struck her. "Did you say your dad is one of the owners of the *Skydome*?"

"So, let me get this straight," Sly said, staring across the booth at Matt. "You and Chloe are calling it quits, we're *not* going to play with the Rockets, and we *are* going to play tomorrow night's dance."

"That's right." Matt's eyes went from Sly to Tony to Jenny. "Sorry I've been ignoring the band lately, guys. I promise, it won't happen again."

Sly wasn't sure whether to be happy or upset. "It's good to have you back, but . . . it would have been *great* to have been able to play with the Rockets. Are you *sure* you want to give up on that?"

"Yes!" Matt, Jenny, and Tony practically shouted the answer at him.

"All right, all right," Sly said. "You don't have to jump all over me."

"I'm glad we're going to play tomorrow's dance," Tony put in. "It's definitely the right thing to do. Do you guys think we could get in some practice time tonight?"

He got up from the booth, tucking in the tails of his Sharkey's work shirt. "Break's over," he said. "I have to get back to work now, but I get off at eight. We could meet after that."

Matt nodded enthusiastically. "Great idea. Maybe we could practice some more tomorrow morning, too."

"Okay," Jenny agreed. She looked up from the newspaper she was holding. "But not too late. I have . . . something I have to do in the afternoon."

Her face had turned red, Sly noticed. Then he saw that her copy of this week's *Clarion* was open to the personals. "Something?" he asked her. "Something . . . *personal* and romantic?"

"Something having to do with Sean Flynn?" Matt added.

Judging from the giddy smile on her face, Matt was right. Sly let out a resigned sigh. It was just his luck that Sean and Jenny would work out their problems instead of breaking up. Sly supposed he was happy for her, but that didn't make it any easier to see her so crazy about some other guy.

"So what if it is," Jenny said. "It's none of your—"

She broke off as the door to Sharkey's flew

open and Tiffani ran in, dragging Lowell by the hand.

"Guess what!" Tiffani cried, hurrying over to their booth. "Lowell is my date today, and—"

"Tiffani, that's great, but you really didn't have to come all the way here to tell us that," Sly cut in, rolling his eyes.

"That's not *all* I have to say," Tiffani said. "You guys, Lowell's father *owns* the Skydome— you know, where the Rockets are going to be playing."

Sly's whole body jerked to attention. "He *does*?"

Lowell nodded. "I just called my dad, and he said that he can arrange it so that California Dreams makes a brief appearance at tomorrow night's show!"

"They already have an opening band, but we could go on, too!" Tiffani added excitedly. "You know, kind of like opening for the opening band."

Sly's mouth fell open. "You're kidding! No, wait a minute, I can tell you're *not* kidding." He whirled around to look at the others. "You guys, this is great!"

He expected everyone to jump out of their skins with joy, but they all just sat there, staring at him.

"Sly, weren't you paying attention to what we were just talking about?" Matt asked.

"Yes, but . . ." Sly started to object but then decided not to. A deal was a deal, after all.

Turning to Lowell, he sighed and said, "Thanks for the offer, but we've already got a gig lined up. We're playing for *The Clarion*'s dance tomorrow night."

Chapter 13

To my California Dream girl,
Please give me a second chance to make your dreams come true. The magic starts at the cove, Saturday at 1 P.M.
Begging for forgiveness, S.

Jenny felt as if she'd been smiling nonstop ever since she first noticed the ad in *The Clarion* yesterday afternoon. Now it was Saturday, at one o'clock, and here she was, at the top of the path that led down to the cove.

Her heart pounded inside her chest as she spotted a sign tacked to a tree next to the path. "This way, Jenny," it read, and there was an arrow pointing down toward the beach.

A few yards farther along, a balloon was tied to a small bush.

"What's this?" Jenny wondered aloud. Beneath the bush was a red, heart-shaped box with a ribbon on it. When she opened up the box, she saw that it was filled with chocolates. A small note with the chocolates read: "More surprises ahead."

Jenny let out a squeal and spun around, hugging herself. She had only gone a dozen feet, and already the magic had begun. She couldn't wait to find out what her next surprise was going to be!

"This time, you'd better be here somewhere, Sean Flynn," she murmured to herself. But even as she said the words, she knew he would be.

She heard his guitar before she actually caught sight of him. When she emerged in the sandy cove, Jenny saw that Sean had spread out a blanket on the sand and was sitting on it, playing his guitar. The sun shone on his face, and the ocean breeze ruffled the golden curls on his forehead.

When Sean saw her, he stopped playing and smiled up at her. "Hi" was all he said, but the look in his eyes told her much more.

"Hi." She grinned and held out the box of chocolates. "I found these on the trail. You don't know who could have put them there, do you?"

Sean shrugged. "Probably some poor slob who's desperate to impress his girlfriend." Shooting her a hopeful glance, he asked, "Did it work?"

She cocked her head to one side and pretended to consider the question. "Well, that depends on what other goodies the poor slob has planned." She sat down cross-legged next to Sean and looked at him expectantly. "I'm waiting," she teased.

"As a matter of fact, I *do* have something," Sean said. Reaching into his pocket, he pulled out a small box and gave it to Jenny. "Go on, open it," he urged.

Jenny didn't have to be told twice. She lifted the lid and then stared in amazement at the gleaming, heart-shaped gold locket and chain glistening against the velvet padding.

"Sean, it's beautiful!" she breathed. "You didn't have to—"

"I wanted to," he interrupted. Taking the locket from its box, he fastened it around her neck. When his fingers touched Jenny's skin, a delicious shiver went through her whole body.

"I'm really going to miss you," Sean said, his voice barely a whisper. "That's why I wanted to give you this—so that you won't forget about me after I move away."

Jenny could feel tears welling up in her eyes. "Sean, I could never forget—"

"*Shhh,*" he said, pressing a finger to her lips. "I don't want us to get sad. This is supposed to be our dream date, remember?" The smile he gave her was so infectious that Jenny couldn't help smiling back. "And I think I know the perfect way to start it."

As Sean leaned over to kiss her, Jenny closed her eyes and pressed hard against him. Everything around her seemed to stop except for the sweet feeling of his lips on hers.

When they finally pulled apart, Jenny nestled her head against his shoulder with a sigh of sheer happiness.

"I don't think anything can totally make up for your moving away," she murmured into his collar. "But this sure comes close."

"Hey, this place looks great!" Matt set down his guitar case and looked around.

The school gym had been completely transformed. Colored lights shone down from the basketball backboards, illuminating the dance floor. Dozens of posters decorated the walls, and there were streamers and balloons everywhere. A bandstand had been set up at the far end of the room, with more spotlights trained on it.

"Randi Jo did a great job," Tony agreed. "And our posters are a knockout, if I do say so myself."

"There's Lowell, over by the bandstand," Tiffani said. "I think I'll go say hi."

Jenny raised an eyebrow. "So is it love between you two?" she asked.

"I'd say *you* have the romance market cornered, based on what you told me about your date today," Tiffani said, grinning at Jenny. "But Lowell is a nice guy. Anyway, I bet he and Randi Jo would appreciate knowing how great everything looks."

Hearing Randi Jo's name, Matt searched her out with his eyes. She was standing next to the long refreshments table, pouring chips into a big bowl. Her long blond hair hung loosely down her back, setting off the blue of her minidress. Gazing at her, Matt felt something twist inside his chest.

"You really miss her, don't you," Jenny said softly.

Matt blinked and turned to find his sister standing right next to him. "I guess I *do*," he admitted. "I was so caught up in trying to play with the Rockets, I didn't even realize what I'd given up." He shot Randi Jo another glance and then sighed. "She used to be my best friend. Now she's practically a stranger, and it's all my fault."

"Maybe you should talk to her, Matt," Jenny suggested.

"I wish I could," he said, frowning. "But she's made it pretty clear that she doesn't want to have anything to do with me."

"That was before you changed your mind

about playing tonight's dance *and* before you and Chloe decided not to go out anymore," Jenny pointed out. "Friends don't just give up on each other. If Randi Jo is still important to you, I think you should at least apologize to her in person. Maybe there's still hope."

Matt glanced over at Randi Jo again. Deep down, he knew Jenny was right. "Thanks for the advice, Sis," he said. "Tell everyone else I'll be over in a minute to set up."

While Jenny took her keyboards over to the platform, Matt headed toward the refreshment table. He was still a few feet away when Randi Jo saw him. She frowned and then turned away and emptied another bag of chips into the bowl on the table.

"Randi Jo, can we talk?" Matt asked. When she didn't say anything right away, he added, "Please? It's important."

She finally looked up at him, and he saw that her blue eyes were troubled and moist. "I don't have anything to say to you. . . ."

"But I have a lot to tell *you*," Matt insisted. "Just hear me out, okay? Then, if you never want to talk to me again, I won't bother you anymore."

For a long moment, Randi Jo just looked at him. "Well . . . okay," she relented.

Randi Jo followed Matt over to a relatively empty part of the gym and climbed up into the bleachers before sitting down and looking at him expectantly. "So, what did you want to tell me?"

Matt took a deep breath. He wished she would smile or say something to help him along, but she just sat in stony silence.

"I don't blame you for being mad at me," he began. "I know I've been really selfish lately. I was really caught up with the Rockets and trying to get the Dreams a gig opening for them. . . . I guess I let it get in the way of our relationship."

"Tell me something I don't already know," Randi Jo grumbled, staring moodily down at her feet.

She wasn't making this any easier for him, but Matt couldn't just give up. He had to try to make her understand. "I thought I wanted more rock and roll in my life, but—"

"You mean, you thought you wanted a rock-and-roll *girl* in your life," Randi Jo cut in. "And I didn't fit the picture. Is that it?"

Matt cringed at the hurt and bitterness in her voice. "It wasn't like that," he insisted. "I just wasn't sure you and I had anything in common anymore. . . ."

"Well, you and Chloe Krieger seem to have plenty in common. I hope you'll be very happy together." Randi Jo stood up and started to climb back down the bleachers, but Matt held her back.

"Wait!" he said urgently. "Randi Jo, I'm trying to apologize here. All I wanted to say is that everything I thought was so important doesn't mean a thing to me if I can't have my friends. I thought California Dreams was worth making *any* sacrifice for. And maybe I *did* think Chloe and I had more in common than you and I, but . . ."

He let out his breath in a rush before continuing. "But I was wrong—about Chloe, about everything. I'm sorry I let you down, and I'm sorry I acted like such a jerk about this dance. I really miss you, Randi Jo. I want us to be together again."

Randi Jo had listened silently while he spoke, her eyes darting over his face. "You're not dating Chloe anymore?" she asked now.

"No," he answered, shaking his head. "She could never mean as much to me as you do."

He smiled at her, and for a moment, he thought Randi Jo would smile back. But then she looked away uneasily.

"I don't know, Matt. I'm not sure things can ever go back to the way they were," she said slowly. "You really hurt me. To tell you the truth, I'm not sure *how* I feel about you anymore."

An unbearable sadness settled in Matt's chest. "Don't you think there's any hope for us to at least be friends? There *has* to be," he insisted. "I mean, I understand if you don't want me to be your boyfriend right now, but I'm going to do whatever it takes to win back your trust and make us friends again." He dropped his voice to a whisper as he added, "There's no way I'm going to lose you altogether, Randi Jo. You mean too much to me."

Matt thought he saw the tense line of her jaw melt just a little. "I guess we could *try* to be friends," she said slowly. "But you have a lot to make up for, Garrison."

Matt was about to respond when Tiffani came rushing up, waving a handful of tickets under Matt's nose. "You guys, check it out! Lowell's dad got us seats for the Rockets' second show—third row center!"

"You're kidding!" Matt's mouth fell open. "It looks like you have enough tickets for every kid at Pacific Coast High!"

"Not quite," Tiffani said, giggling. "But we do have enough for everyone in the Dreams, plus Sean, and Lowell, and you, Randi Jo. I'm psyched!"

Matt turned to Randi Jo and gave her his most persuasive smile. "What do you say?" he asked. "Will you come with me? As friends?"

The corners of Randi Jo's mouth lifted in a return smile. "Sure." She reached over and gave his hand a squeeze. "As friends."